Layers

By
AlTonya Washington

LAYERS
Copyright© by AlTonya Washington

ISBN: 9781452864372

Printed in USA by CreateSpace

Book I

Layers of Trouble

LLL

"Stop it," Kamari Grade ordered without so much as a glimpse across her shoulder. Stepping closer to the elevator's chrome paneling, she squinted to take a better look at the unruly auburn curls covering her head. Kamari felt her back stiffen when she heard another sigh that was given purely for spite.

"Screw you Kam," Eliza Breck hissed, folding her arms as best she could over her ample bust line. "It's not *your* family who's about to start hating you-again."

"They don't hate you."

"They will," Eliza sang.

Having been a participant in the familiar argument more times than she cared to admit, Kam nodded and went back to checking her reflection in the elevator's chrome.

"First they tell me to get some people in here to do pieces for positive press on the company." Eliza recalled, scowling at the overhead numbers flashing each floor the car approached. "I don't have to remind you what a mess that was."

"You didn't know he was a reporter," Kam broke her vow of silence then.

"Now I'm about to ruin what could be our one shot at climbing out of this latest financial crap storm." Eliza added as though her best friend had never spoken.

By now, Kamari accepted that the familiar argument regarding Eliza's relationship with her family would take place as usual. "Exactly how does preventing them from becoming involved with a financial monster equal out to be *your* fault?"

"Money men aren't exactly chomping at the bit to help us, you know?" Eliza snapped, her blue eyes fierce with agitation and apprehension. "Huron Base might have a reputation as a shark, but God knows the man's got money. Bringing you in on this might sour the whole deal-that means no money, company in financial upheaval-*again* and yours truly at fault for more unrest *again!*"

"Dammit Eliza why the hell did you come to me then?!"

"Because you're the best," Eliza admitted through clenched teeth. "Still, I guess I didn't expect you to find as much as you did. Guess I underestimated how good you really are."

In spite of her own agitated state, Kamari took a moment to bask in the accolade. Of course, it was well deserved. In the field of troubleshooting investigation, the phrase Kamari Grade was almost universal. Not only was it her name, but it had become a standard by which all others in her profession were judged.

To look at her, one would never think the petite caramel colored beauty with her head full of glossy reddish curls could be likened to a ravenous wolf on the scent of a kill. The comparison fit Kam perfectly when it came to getting the goods on a business that was less than worthy of her clients trust.

"In spite of how good I am," Kam sighed once she'd come from under the haze of self-adoration, "your family's under no obligation to take my advice-they may still sign with Surge Five in spite of the fact that it's owned by Huron Base. You'll have the money and mommy and daddy will still tuck you in tonight."

"Go screw yourself Kam."

"No more appealing than it was the first time you suggested it." Kam muttered, her attention focusing on a wayward string dangling from the faux jacket pocket of her baby blue pantsuit.

"The last thing this company needs is to be linked to someone with a sinister rep like Huron Base."

It was true. Breck Industries had more than their fair share of scandals. It was usually the case with companies that could trace establishment dates back to the turn of the twentieth century. Even still, Breck managed to stand out among those with the more unfortunate and shameful pasts. The black marks against the company included everything from takeovers from within and scores of sexual harassment suits, to company espionage and embezzlement. Hence one financial struggle after another.

Huron Base could put an end to that, Kam acknowledged. Her breath caught in her throat as the lengthy elevator ascent reached its conclusion. Yes, Huron Base's seemingly unending supply of gravy trains could've squashed the Breck's latest blemish without breaking stride.

Huron Base was an unstoppable and almost frightening force in the world of finance. The juvenile delinquent with a creative and lengthy record had revamped his life and his lifestyle. He'd become a man respected, admired and revered in the world he claimed dominance over. It had once been said that numbers laid down for him and money fell at his feet as helplessly as the women who craved just a moment of his time. Rumors boasted that his simple presence was enough to close a deal. All that high powered raving sent a shrill of delight along Kamari's spine-she got to be the one to take the powerful giant down a notch.

***

"Kamari!" Garrick and Jessica Breck were the first members of the family to rush forward and envelop their daughter's best friend in a warm hug.

"When El finally broke her silence and told us all that she'd hired you to look into the backgrounds of our possible lenders, we knew we'd gotten the cream of the crop." Samuel Breck, Eliza's uncle said while kissing Kamari's cheek.

Kam risked a wilting glance at her friend who was being hugged and kissed by her parents. Eliza had been right of course. Her report on Huron Base's anonymously owned company could be the Breck's deciding factor. Either they weren't in a hurry to do business with Surge Five or they didn't think she'd come across any negatives in her investigation. Final report meetings never riled her, but this one had her shaking in her four inch pumps.

"Let's get started then," Simon Breck called, waving the group to the long polished cherry wood table in the far corner of the well-lit room.

Aside from Eliza and well...herself, Kam could see that Simon wasn't looking forward to the meeting either. Not surprising. Her search had uncovered Simon and Huron Base ran in similar...recreational circles. They'd developed a friendship and Kam was certain that accounted for Simon approaching his family about doing business with Surge Five.

Garrick Breck nodded toward Kam. "We won't waste time with formalities love. Whenever you're ready."

"Right," Kam cleared her throat and opened the folder she carried. She knew the contents by heart, but needed another few moments to make sure her thoughts were on accord with her voice. "You already know what's on the surface of Surge Five's business statement and stock portfolios. That's all on the level...but beneath that glossy layer I've discovered that the company is owned by Huron Base."

"Base?" Coyt Breck whispered.

Kamari nodded toward the eldest of the Breck brothers. "It seems Mr. Base owns several corporations-none of which he claims to own outright."

"Well what's he hiding?" Garrick asked.

"Well sir, this *is* Huron Base we're discussing," Kam reminded the man softly. "It wasn't a huge shock to me. After all, a man with Mr. Base's background understands that certain clients would shy away from him."

"And clearly it's not that many who shy away," Simon spoke up then.

"Continue love," Garrick Breck instructed smoothly, overlooking his nephew's observation.

Clearing her throat, Kam continued her report. There was no way she could talk about Huron Base without shining light on his numerous and successful holdings. It went without saying that any company would give its right...whatever to have Huron Base and his wealth in its corner.

The problem? Huron Base always demanded controlling interest over monetary payment. The man's clients ranged from the most wholesome franchises to powerful conglomerates built on foundations of blood and bone. Kam had uncovered all this in spite of the layers of gloss Huron's more suspect corporations had managed to acquire over the years. She knew anyone's history was possible to acquire if the one looking had a close personal friendship with layers. Layers were beautiful and enough of them could hide the ugliest parts of ones history.

A company like Breck Industries-with a history muddled in scandal, certainly didn't need bonds with a financier who kept monstrous organizations in business.

"Who's next on the list after Surge Five?"

"Ah come on!" Simon snapped finally and pounded a clenched fist to the hard table. "You're saying no, because of that report?!"

Samuel Breck leaned forward to glower at his son. "Because of Huron Base. We've got enough problems without bringing him in."

"Newsflash dad, there aren't that many trying to jump to the head of the line to bail us out, you know?"

"I think we're pretty much in agreement that there will be no business with Surge Five."

"No! Hell no!" Simon blared, flushing sharply beneath the deep tan of his skin. "You old fools are gonna run this company straight into the ground," he promised Coyt who had spoken.

"Kamari dear, thank you for this report. You've done a fine job-we thank you for delving deep enough to find what we needed." Garrick said, while standing.

Risking a meaningful look at Eliza, Kam acknowledged that her friend would not have a delightful morning. Eliza appeared tense enough to deflect the path of a bullet. Her skin was a pale as the airy cream skirt suit she wore.

"We're still on for lunch." Eliza spoke through clenched teeth.

Kam knew that meant a heavy round of drinks would be in order. She squeezed her friend's shoulder then followed Garrick Breck to the boardroom door.

***

After the meeting, Kam ran a few errands and stopped by her office shortly after eleven-thirty. Dedicated to a fault, she always made a point of stopping in to check on things even if she had no plans to work inside that day.

Tenille Yancy appeared relieved and uneasy the moment her boss strolled from the elevator. "You've got a um…guest."

Surprised by the oversight, Kam didn't take notice of her assistant's edginess. Instead, she reached for her Blackberry to check her schedule.

"Oh he-he's not on any of your schedules." Tenille stood from her desk chair when Kam fixed her with a raised eyebrow. "I told him you weren't expected today. He said he'd wait a while."

"In my office?"

"Uh-huh."

Replacing the Blackberry in her gray tote, Kam stood back to observe the harried young woman. "Dare I hope you got his name?"

"He um…he didn't give it," Tenille's lashes fluttered with maddening speed. "Oh Kam, I'm sorry. He was just so persuasive and so…beautiful."

Now both Kam's brows arched. "Beautiful?"

"Mmm."

"Tenille!"

"Sorry," the girl hissed, trailing a shaking hand across her brow.

Moving closer to the desk, Kam took a more studious look at her assistant. It was pretty easy to spot the tension that was about far more than letting an unnamed, unexpected and...beautiful guest into her office.

"When's Blake due for leave?" Kam asked, perching on the edge of the neat white oak desk.

Tenille almost laughed amidst her misery. "*Leave*," she repeated the word as though it put a bad taste in her mouth. "With more soldiers being deployed everyday who's to say when I'll see my husband again-*if* I'll see him..."

Kam wouldn't hug her knowing it would only make the pain spear deeper. Instead, she picked up a folder and tapped it to the sleeve of Tenille's mauve blouse.

"Take off," Kam ordered, smiling when the girl's brows drew close. "I want you to get out of here. Grab some movies from the store, get your toes done, get your favorite ice cream or chocolates or whatever the hell makes you feel good and start your weekend early."

Tenille leaned back in the chair, her brown eyes misty with sudden tears. "You're too good to me Kam."

"No," Kam groaned, sounding far older than her thirty-one years. "I just understand the ugliness of sexual frustration." She admitted and laughed when Tenille rounded the desk and kissed her cheek.

It took her assistant less than two minutes to clear out. All the humor and light left with Tenille. Then, Kam put her most unwelcoming expression in place and prepared to meet her mystery guest.

He was built, she'd give him that. Of course, it was about *all* she could give him since he was presently seated with his back to the door and perched on the corner of her desk. He was conducting a phone conversation while gazing serenely at her view of San Francisco Bay as he spoke. When Kamari slammed the door, he didn't even have the decency to look over his shoulder.

"See you around three Jaysun," he said, the depth of his voice growing softer as he smoothly ended the call. He tapped the cell once against his thigh covered by mocha trousers and turned.

Kamari cleared her throat in a reflexive gesture. Her intention was to dislodge her heart where it had made a stunning leap from her chest. Calling a man beautiful was at the very end of that long list of things she swore she'd never do. Ever. But she'd be damned if this man wasn't precisely that.

Aside from the six foot plus muscular build which was more massive than lean, his appearance was alluring in every sense of the word. The caramel skin was the same tone as hers and, dammit, just as flawless. Close cut midnight hair waved across his head and he wore the sleek black beard just as close cut. The affect cast a shadow across his face which accentuated his coaxing and purely dangerous appeal.

Kam rolled her eyes while giving herself a mental kick. *Get your head out of your panties*, she ordered and stepped forward.

"Kamari Grade?" He asked, keeping his spot on the end of her desk.

She shrugged. "I better be or else my assistant's prized skills of preventing unwanted visitors inside my office are rapidly deteriorating." She countered firmly, while willing everything inside her to stop throbbing.

Sleek brows rose over deep set and potently seductive green eyes. The color was as surprising as it was unsettling. Fringed by unfairly long lashes, they added an element that kept him from appearing too fierce but no less dangerous. At that moment, he looked as though he'd come expecting one thing and had been pleasantly surprised to find another. He set down his phone as though it were an afterthought and stood.

"Huron Base." He said.

Of course you are, Kam acknowledged silently. She recalled her agitation over not being able to find a picture of him during the investigation. Now she celebrated the set back. Looks like that only distracted *and aroused*. She'd have never completed her investigation.

"Well this *is* a surprise, Mr. Base. Most people just send nasty emails or ugly flowers with ugly notes to tell me what they think of me," she spoke in a phony tone of admiration while tapping one of her chic peek-a-boo pumps to the carpet. "Never had anyone visit me personally to do it."

"I like to look into the eyes of my adversaries," he admitted, though it was clear that he'd come to look at much more.

Kam rolled her eyes. "Well the next time, make an appointment to do it," she advised and bristled as his brilliant stare leered more intensely.

"Forgive me. Simon called to tell me the deal fell through. I was stunned when he told me about your report." Hiding his hands in his trouser pockets he nodded as if commending her. "Most people glimpse the annual earnings of my companies and don't bother to look farther."

"It's my job to get past all the gloss," she said, her lips parting on the threshold of a smile.

Huron took a moment to respond. His gaze locked on her full, kissable mouth and every thought vanished from his mind.

"Mr. Base?" Kamari prompted.

"You say 'gloss' like it's a bad word," he managed to respond that time.

"Gloss is a lovely word that usually hides many ugly things."

"Like me?"

"Like what you do."

"Mmm hmm," he returned with a smile. The look in his eyes though was anything but humorous.

Kam believed her emotions mingled with a bit of what a maiden might feel in the domain of a dangerous pirate. Inside, she called herself a fool over the comparison. Still, the way he watched her-smiling but with that underlying intensity. It was a patient intensity that said he knew she'd resist whatever he wanted to discover about her. Moreover, it would take a great deal of time to...persuade her-and he was ready for the challenge.

But he could wait, Huron decided. He *would* wait. He'd never know if meeting her beforehand may have influenced her report in his favor. Somehow he didn't think it would have. Still, he was intrigued by her, mostly because she didn't appear to be intrigued by *him*. Aside from all that, what man could resist wanting to know the tough, tiny caramel beauty?

"If you're done Mr. Base, I'm a very busy person." Kam blurted, not wanting the man to see how affected she was becoming by his incessant staring.

Huron grinned, watching as she appeared to be heading in the direction of her desk but couldn't remember what to do once she got there. On top of that, the provocative fit of the pantsuit revealed that she was slightly bow-legged. Now he really had no choice but to see her again. After all, what man could resist a tough, tiny, caramel, *slightly bow-legged* beauty?

"I apologize for taking up so much of your time. I only wanted to meet you," he said and suddenly moved close to extend his hand for shaking.

It was a move that often caused most men to tremble. Primarily, it was due to his size and the element of danger that; he'd once been told, almost clung to him. Kamari didn't as much as blink and it was Huron who almost forgot to let go of her hand.

In fact, Kam didn't move until she was alone in her office. It was then that she remembered to sit behind her desk. She began browsing a few documents Tenille had left for her to sign. Then, she dropped the act and began to fan the papers before her face.
***
"He just stormed out like that?"

"Well, the storming out came after a cursing tirade and a few chairs being slammed against the wall."

"Jesus."

Eliza tossed back what remained of the third Cosmopolitan she'd ordered following lunch with Kamari. "I'm afraid for Simon-for my family's company, but especially for Simon."

"Shh..." Kam patted her friend's hand where it trembled on the stem of the glass. "He'll be fine. Just a little on edge right now is all."

Eliza was shaking her head. The clipped blonde waves of her hair thrashed around her shoulders. "You don't get it. If they turn their backs on him...even with their support he can barely maintain his lifestyle. There's gambling and...I know there's some other illegal stuff too."

"Shh..." Kamari urged, though she was starting to wonder if Simon Breck's background couldn't stand a bit of investigating.

Eliza drained the rest of her Cosmopolitan then dutifully got started on the steaming mug of creamy coffee the waiter had just set down. "Sorry to be such a drag," she apologized mid-sip.

"Shut up," Kam ordered, still working on her second Long Island Iced Tea.

"No really," Eliza tucked a strand behind her ear and studied her friend. "You didn't look all that pepped-up when I walked in here earlier."

Laughing shortly, Kam leaned back against the booth. "Hell, I wasn't. Huron Base was waiting in my office when I went by after the meeting."

Hearing the man's name did more to sober up Eliza than the coffee. "What's he like?" she whispered in an almost reverent tone.

"I think the word Tenille used was 'beautiful'," Kam replied and then took a quick sip of her drink to wash down a sudden rise of bile.

"Hmph. Yeah...that's what I heard."

"What you *heard*?" Kam fixed her best friend with a disgusted stare.

"Well, I didn't know for sure. You know how women talk. Shit Kam, I never met him!" Eliza snapped, tiring of the daggers being fired at her. She shrugged. "I couldn't believe you found out he and Simon were so close. I don't think I've ever seen them together."

Kam swallowed the rest of her drink. "I don't think their social circles are exactly your thing."

"So what did he say to you?"

"Not what you'd expect. Said he came to look into the eyes of his adversary," she drawled with a flip wave of her hand. "I was prepared for a battle that never came." Kam admitted, though silently she wondered if Huron Base's style of battle was just too suave to pin down.

"You know you haven't seen the last of him?" Eliza predicted, patting Kam's shoulder when she shuddered.

A moment later, the subtle hum of a vibrating cell phone sent both women searching their bags. Eliza emerged the victor only to discover she was being summoned back to the office.

Kamari was about to try her luck at sobering up. She raised her hand to signal the waiter for coffee when her eyes narrowed towards the front of the bakery café.

I'll be damned. The words thudded like a stone in her head while she stared at Huron Base. She listened to him tease with the owner's wife and order a spinach quiche. Then Kam decided enough was enough.

"If I were a paranoid woman, I'd swear you were following me."

Huron turned and sleek brows rose in a show of instant satisfaction. "Kamari..." he seemed to sigh while smirking at the agitation that seemed to flash on her face.

"What are you doing in here?"

His laughter turned the heads of several women, yet his striking gaze remained focused on Kamari. "This is one of my favorite places."

"Bull."

"I swear."

"Mmm I'm about to."

"I'm not lying. I promise you," he said then, pressing a hand to the front of his suit coat. "I stop by every other day for the spinach quiche. Isn't that right, Ms. V?"

Vanessa Hale smiled while ringing up Huron's sale. "That's right," she sang.

Kam didn't bother to argue, but silently decided the man could coax a woman into saying anything he desired.

"Is this to go, Hon?" Vanessa Hale was asking Huron.

He looked back at Kam. "Are you coming or going?"

"Going, but don't base your answer on me," she added with a quick wave of her hand.

"It's to go Ms. V," Huron replied, his eyes still locked on Kamari's face. "Can I take you somewhere?" he asked, leaning against the glass counter while his quiche was packed.

"No thanks," she whispered polite yet firmly while handing her check to the clerk at the other end of the counter.

"What if I insisted?"

"Then I'd *insist* on saying no."

"Well there's no way I can let you drive," he decided and rose to his full height.

Kam managed to keep her smile sweet while accepting her change from the clerk. The sweetness faded when she turned to frown up into Huron's dashing face. "Look-"

"No way are you driving when I can smell the Long Islands on your clothes," he challenged, trying to keep his mind off how delightfully her clothes fit her tiny frame.

"I'm *not* driving, I-" Kam stopped to grab hold to her rising temper. "I'm not driving, I'm walking."

Huron was leaning over the counter to kiss Vanessa Hale's cheek once she'd passed him the quiche. "Well I'd say walking is just as dangerous as driving in your condition," he countered and brushed the back of his hand along her arm before waving it before her. "Shall we?"

Just give in Kam, maybe he'll be bored by how easy it was to get you in his car and you'll be rid of him. While the reasoning did little to convince her, she was too weary to argue any more that day.

"Quiche?" Huron offered once they were settled in the dark interior of the sleek Limo that waited outside the café.

She closed her eyes momentarily. "I've eaten, Mr. Base."

"It's Huron, Kami."

She bristled at the way his rich brogue cradled her name. "Don't call me Kami, *Huron.*"

"It suits you," he argued, facing her more fully on the suede back seat.

Ensconced in the soothing dark with his towering muscular frame subtly crowding her, Kamari refused to show any response. Instead, she focused on the passing beauty of downtown San Francisco and prayed he couldn't hear the tiny moans trying to rise from her chest.

"Come on just let me give you a little. I promise you won't regret making room for it."

One of the pesky moans escaped then. Kam wouldn't amuse him further by reacting to his intentionally suggestive remark.

Smiling when he saw her reluctant nod, Huron forked off an ample portion and brought the utensil within inches of Kam's mouth. She moved to reach for the fork and wasn't surprised to discover he wanted to feed her.

Make it easy, the tiny voice advised again. Kam agreed to do so as long as he didn't try giving her anything more than food.

The quiche was of course, heavenly. She felt every delectable ingredient burst to life inside her mouth and couldn't resist the second, third and fourth forkful he offered.

"You sure?" he prompted when she waved off more. "So were you eating alone at the café?"

"No. Lunch with a friend."

The split-second tightening of a jaw muscle surprised Huron. Her innocent confession had sent a shudder of something fierce through his chest. "How long have you lived here?" he asked to cover his frustration.

"Since after college," Kam shared and rested her head back along the seat.

"Where from originally?" Huron asked, helping himself to a monstrous serving of the quiche.

"Colorado. Denver. My parents live in Aspen now," she said and laughed at his stunned expression.

"Lucky them," he said, his gaze lingering a bit when she shrugged. "Well, I guess there's no point in *my* sharing. You know all there is."

"And that's not even half way true."

He had the decency to grin. "You know I come from the streets. I've got a record a mile long-"

"I wouldn't say a mile."

"For a black man, an inch is too long."

Kam nodded in silent agreement.

"...you know about all my dark dealings-ones that have given me a pretty scary image."

Kam studied his build and the beauty of his profile. "I think you sort of like that scary image."

"Shh...we don't want the whole world to know, do we?" He teased, allowing his expression to become a tad serious then. "Being thought of as scary is a handy weapon in business. It's murder in a personal life," he admitted and then smirked and raised his quiche. "More?" he invited.

Kam wasted no time accepting.

Conversation moved along in an unforced and unhurried manner. Kam only revealed a little more about herself-two could play that game. Besides, she was still a little too buzzed to carry a larger load of the discussion. She admitted rather reluctantly, that she was far more interested in hearing *his* story. Of course, he didn't reveal much more than she'd uncovered in her files. Either he craved his privacy or the contents of his private past were too dark to be revealed to a new acquaintance.

For Huron, it was a mixture of both. Losing the Breck deal was unfortunate, for many reasons, but it wasn't the first deal he'd lost. It certainly wasn't the first deal he'd ever lost because of his background. But he'd never lost to a woman like Kamari Grade. Hell, he'd never lost to a woman-period. He thought back to the earlier question he'd posed-would her findings on him have been so inflammatory had he met her first and had the chance to... persuade her? The answer was no, she'd have batted those beautiful eyes at him and gone right ahead with the damning report.

He never saw her coming and she'd counted on that. She was good-damned good at her job and she knew it. Still, she hadn't found any more on him than he'd allow. That surprised him, given her professional reputation. It also relieved him, for the contents of his private past were indeed too dark to be revealed to a new acquaintance. She was a new acquaintance he believed he'd very much enjoy getting to know far better. If she uncovered the layers of his past, he could forget that ever happening.

Realizing he'd gotten lost in an unexpectedly deep sea of thought, Huron cleared his throat and prepared to deliver a ready explanation. Instead, he discovered his riding companion could've cared less.

Kam was slumped to one side along the seat, head bowed, eyes closed and lips slightly parted. Huron tilted his head to study her a bit more closely. God, she was a beauty. He'd give anything to know where that red hair came from and if it was natural... Clearing his throat, he decided that was a topic best left alone-for the time being. Besides, his sudden and surprising attraction for her was more than skin deep. His first impression of her shrieked everything he loved about his life-challenge, drive, determination, ease, strength, sexiness and beauty. For a man who could acquire anything, the allure of such a conquest was a thing he couldn't let pass by.

"Graham?" Huron greeted his driver through the car phone. "Let's take Ms. Grade home instead," he decided, praying once they got there he'd be gentleman enough to put her to bed and let her be.

***

Kam woke with a start and blinked. She'd been dreaming of bells. It took her only a brief moment to realize she was at home in her own bed and yet another moment to experience relief over the fact that she was alone. Smoothing a hand along her body, more relief flooded when she felt her clothes were still in place. Still, she was left with one-perhaps two nagging questions. What happened in that car once she...drifted off and what happened when Huron brought her to bed. In spite of her imbibed state, she was sure he'd carried her from his car.

Hissing a curse, Kam decided she was overreacting. More relief flooded her system, but not enough to completely put her at ease. When the phone rang, she celebrated the intrusion on her cluttered thoughts.

"Kam?!"

"Yes? Eliza?"

"Kam, thank God! Where the hell have you been? I've been calling for the past hour!"

That explained the bell dream, but not why her best friend was screaming like a banshee. "Eliza, just calm down-"

"I need you here, Kam."

"Where are you?"

"The office. The office...oh God Kam..."

"Eliza? Eliza?! Calm down and tell me what-"

"He's dead. He's dead Kam-oh God..."

"Who? Eliza-"

"Simon. My cousin is dead."

***

Simon Breck was not only dead he'd been killed-murdered in his office. Eliza had found her cousin when she went to speak with him about the day's events. Nothing could've prepared her to find Simon in his desk chair with two shots to his forehead and one to his temple.

The entire building was like a madhouse. The executive floor was a madhouse to the hundredth power. A half hour passed before Kam found her friend. The detectives on scene had wanted to speak with Kam regarding that morning's meeting. No one was spouting names of possible suspects, but clearly what went on in that meeting was of the highest importance. A sinking feeling began to churn in the pit of Kam's stomach.

God was this her fault? She tried to shake off the notion, but couldn't. Sure it wasn't the first time she'd ever second guessed what she did for a living. Troubleshooting was a nasty business and her prized investigations could either make or break a company. Over the years, she'd amassed her fair share of enemies. Part of the game, she told herself. Unfortunately, nothing prepared her for someone dying because of a report. Moreover, nothing prepared her for that someone to be part of her best friend's family.

Still, Eliza needed her and that had to count for something. She and Eliza had been friends since college and Kamari didn't think she'd survive it if anything happened to jeopardize that. Besides, none of the other family members had spit in her face yet so Kam latched onto the hope that Simon's demise had no link to the Base deal falling through.

A uniformed officer was escorting her to Eliza, when Kam's toe-hold on hope evaporated. Huron Base stood at the end of a long corridor speaking with two men Kam recognized as Coyt and Samuel Breck. He looked in her direction as if sensing her presence. His expression should have reduced her to nothing.

Gone was the soft, subtle hint of desire she'd glimpsed earlier in his striking jade stare. His look held all the considerable rage she was sure simmered below the surface of his powerful frame. So much for asking what happened in her apartment. He'd probably rip out her throat for reminding him that he'd ever touched her-or wanted to.

The officer spoke her name and Kam managed a nod before following the woman on through. She pressed her lips together-stunned to feel them trembling in the wake of a sob.

***

"What are you doing here Kam?" she asked herself for what had to be the fifth time since she'd parked her truck on the street outside Huron Base's San Francisco office. It had been four days since the Simon Breck murder. In that time, she'd almost gone crazy trying to keep Eliza from going over the ragged edge with fear over what she'd seen.

Kamari trailed shaking fingers through her reddish curls and sighed. She'd been close to the ragged edge herself and knew what she was about to do might be just the thing to push her right on over.

But he wasn't at the funeral and she...what? Missed him? *God Kam, what are you doing?* Again, the question filtered to the surface. Whatever the circumstances, Simon Breck and Huron Base had been close friends. It was only right that she pay her respects.

Good one, Kam.

"Shut up," she hissed at the voice and left the Nissan Titan.

The top floor was quieter than a morgue. Not a cheery, self-soothing acknowledgement, but it was true. Kam idled by the receptionist's desk for almost five minutes before daring to move on to the President's wing. She wasn't surprised to see the executive assistant's desk vacant and squared her shoulders while heading for the only office on the lengthy corridor.

A sense of déjà vu intruded when she stepped to the open doorway. Once her shock at the mammoth size of the office drained, she focused on the man she'd come to see. He clearly had no trouble sitting with his back to an open door for there he was perched comfortably on the edge of a huge, rather cluttered desk with a phone receiver nestled in the crook of his neck. Before him, there was a jaw-dropping view of the Pacific.

Why does it matter if you tell him you're sorry about his friend Kam? She knew the answer, but didn't want to speak it. Alright, alright...so she missed him. Dammit.

Huron turned then and Kamari couldn't help but wonder if he'd been waiting for her to voice the admission in her mind.

"Call you back Rich," he told the person on the line and tossed the cordless receiver somewhere atop the folder and paper-ridden desk. "Kami," he greeted.

Her eyes threatened to close as the soothing brogue of his heavy voice filled the spacious room. Barely, she managed to clear her throat and urged her pump-shod feet forward.

Huron stood, watching as she motioned towards the hallway. She bit her lip in a manner that was so innocently alluring, he envisioned himself taking her until they were both too spent to move.

"Sorry to bother you, there was no one out-"

"It's alright," he promised, green eyes narrowing as they raked the wispy olive dress that flared about her legs and gloved her tiny, provocative frame. "Are you okay?"

Speak! She commanded herself. Wondering what it was about the man and praying she'd not suddenly developed a craving for former bad boys who still wore their thug4life mentality like a shroud.

"Kamari?" Huron called again, now appearing as if he were actually worried.

"I'm fine," she blurted and waved both her hands. "I'm okay, I just..."

Pushing one hand into a deep pocket of his silver gray trousers, Huron leaned close. "Just?" he prompted.

"I-" she trailed away as everything she'd been forcing herself not to feel relentlessly swirled inside her. "I um..." she tried.

Grinning the slow easy grin that was part danger, part persuasion and completely sexy, Huron sealed whatever distance remained between them. Kam stood on her toes in anticipation of being kissed before he even bowed his head. Huron didn't disappoint.

The act wasn't pounding and savage as she'd expected. Instead, it draped a sensation over her entire body-lilting like the finest fabric. Lightly, her hands rested on the wall of his chest while his arm linked smoothly around her waist. Kam heard her moans filling the office, but didn't care. His tongue delved, caressed and stroked her mouth all in a gentle, coaxing manner that sent every part of her tingling.

The kiss was as persuasive as his words and Kamari accepted defeat as she arched into his granite frame. Sliding her hands across the crisp material of the dark blue shirt he wore, she tried to stand on the very tips of her toes to reach him more comfortably. Ceasing her torment, Huron simply leaned down and scooped her up neatly against him. He tilted his head, kissing her from another angle and felt a surge of arrogant confidence when a tortured sigh reached his ears. Kam reciprocated when he applied teasing quick pecks to her mouth before he ended the kiss.

"Did we sleep together?" she moaned the second her lips were free.

A quick smirk curved his mouth, but Huron masked it easily. For a while, he studied her-the gorgeous brown eyes-soft with desire, the small hands curled into half fists against his chest as her breasts heaved against it. Her mouth...God her mouth beckoned his for another kiss. Unknowingly, the delectable woman in his arms had sealed her fate. She'd hitched a ride on his possessive streak and Huron was sure he'd never let her off.

"You mean you don't remember?" he asked then, deciding to toy with her for a time.

The gorgeous brows widened in horror and Kam tried desperately to swallow once she'd croaked out the words. "Oh God..."

"Is it such a bad thing, Kami?" he queried in a phony, offended tone of voice.

"I don't know you," she blurted and took stock of her position. "Yet here I am in your office, kissing you like a mad woman, panties soaked-oh no..." she moaned again, realizing she'd served up a bit too much information.

Huron laughed and silently admitted how long it had been since he'd really done so. She was absolutely too much the way he wanted her. *God help me if I ever fall in love with her.* Shaking his head as if to clear it; he gave a little squeeze which brought her eyes back to his face.

"Nothing happened," he assured her. "You passed out-fell asleep," he rephrased when her eyes narrowed threateningly. "I took you to your apartment put you to bed...I didn't see or touch anything." He added with an adorably innocent smile.

Her body lost a bit of its rigidity. "You could've done anything," she said almost to herself.

"You were asleep. What's the fun in that?" Huron challenged, although he was more than aware of the fact. After all, hadn't he spent the last week calling himself all sorts of fools for not taking at least one peek at the lush body presently nestled against him? "Trust me," he soothed, allowing her to slide down to length of him, "When we sleep together you'll damn well remember it."

Kam felt her heart pounding in her ears and prayed her feet would support her trip to the door. "I should go," she whispered, waving a hand behind her.

"Kami?" Huron called, just as her hand brushed the jamb.

She watched him slant a gaze to a chair and realized she was about to leave without her purse.

"Did you drive?" he asked as she turned to leave again.

Fixing him with a blank look, Kam simply nodded.

Huron walked toward her and shut the heavy door with barely a flick of his wrist.

"Why don't you wait a while?" he suggested.

Kam rolled her eyes. "I'm fine, just a little drained." *And fabulously aroused*, the words sang in her head.

Huron shook his head and led her to one of the large, deep black chairs set around his large stone desk. "Humor me, hmm? I don't trust you to get there in one piece and I already buried one acquaintance this week."

Kam felt her lips thin and remember her *real* reason for stopping by. "He was your friend." She acknowledged.

"A good one," Huron admitted with a somber nod.

"I wanted to tell you how sorry I was."

Huron's expression still masked unrest. "I'm sorry too. In spite of it all, he was a good man-didn't deserve to go down like that. Came to me for help," he shook his head. "God, he was desperate-he'd had a gambling problem for years. Finally put his family's company in jeopardy because of it." Huron leaned against his desk and trailed a thumb across the dimple in his chin. "Obviously, he didn't want his family to know, but he knew they would if another financier came in to scan the books."

Kam leaned forward in the chair, her lips parting in amazement. "You were trying to help him."

Huron shrugged. "I didn't do a very good job."

"Because of me."

"What?"

"You blame me."

"Kamari no-"

"Hell, *I* blame me. If it weren't for my investigation-"

"Stop. Stop now." The order was firm as he left the desk to kneel next to the chair she occupied. "Why would you think I blame you?"

She didn't want to answer, but had no choice once he'd hooked a hand below her knee and turned her to face him.

"I saw the way you looked at me. When I saw you at Breck afterwards…" she added when he watched her in bewilderment. "You were talking with Simon's father and uncle."

"Jesus," Huron breathed, covering his face with one hand. When he lowered it, he was smiling. "That had nothin' to do with you, Babe."

"You looked right at me," she argued.

He chuckled. "No offence, but it's almost impossible for me not to."

Instantly, Kam bowed her head when the heat bloomed in her cheeks.

He leaned closer to peer into her eyes. "I'm sorry," he said and watched in helpless fascination as she trailed a hand through an abundance of reddish-brown curls.

"I actually went to the bathroom and cried. No man ever made me cry," she revealed and then rolled her eyes in disgust. "I can't believe I told you that," she hissed before slapping both hands to her thighs. "Well hey you can put that down on your list of successes-'making a nosy little troubleshooting bitch cry like a baby'."

Huron caught both her hands in one of his and squeezed. "Don't do that."

Kam looked away. She didn't want him to be nice to her. She'd never be able to resist what he made her feel-made her *want*-if he was nice to her.

"Sorry I barged in like this," she said, smiling softly when he gave over her purse. She slid off the chair and left Huron Base still kneeling next to it.

***

Kamari managed to put in a decent days work the following day. Around six, she felt she'd pretended long enough and drove thirty five minutes to Breck Tower. Of course, Eliza had reserved a spot right at the front of her thoughts-right next to Huron Base that is.

Closing her eyes briefly, Kam spared a minute to dwell on what happened in his office the night before. Was she crazy? Getting involved with someone she'd investigated was about the most foolish thing she could do. In a business like hers, such a weakness could damage more than her reputation. It could damage her heart. She'd been through far too much to take the fragile muscle through any more torment.

After all, how many suave sexy men had she met during her years as an investigative troubleshooter? Tons. *Come off it Kam*, the voice of reason spat. Never had she come across a man like Huron Base. The men she'd met in the course of her work were usually polished in word and deed. Aside from offers to dinner or drinks, none of them had ever swooped in and coaxed her into intimate limo rides or heated office interludes. And never had one been inside her home.

There was a seductive arrogance to Huron that blared former thug. The danger lay in the fact that the image didn't seem to be one he completely wished to shed. In spite of the luxury now surrounding him, she could almost feel the deadly part of his persona surging beneath the layer of gloss he sported like a lovely accessory.

He's got to know this would never work, she tried to assure herself. *But wouldn't you love to know if it could?* Kam refused to entertain an answer. She was pulling into the underground garage at Breck and decided to leave thoughts of her strange involvement with Huron Base in the car.

"El?" Kam called. The girl hadn't been in her office and Kamari was momentarily relieved, hoping she'd gone home for the day. When Kam heard a thud followed by a high-pitched female curse, she went to investigate.

"Eliza?" Kam called again stepping into the conference room.

Eliza was seated at the head of the long cherry-wood table which was presently cluttered with scores of papers and folders.

"Kam, thank God." Eliza muttered, sparing a brief glimpse in her friend's direction. "I'm hitting a brick wall here."

"With what?" Kam inquired slowly, taking stock of the papers her friend shuffled.

Eliza trailed a hand through her glossy waves and rolled her eyes. "Something I remembered…from the meeting after you left that day."

Kam took a seat in one of the chairs closest to the head of the table. "What was it?"

"When the arguing began…" Eliza trailed away, looking as if she were trying to get her thoughts in order before speaking again. "I need you to do something that may be illegal."

Kam tilted her head. "Something."

"Check financial records outlaying money to a Dr. Christine Daily."

Folding her arms across the short waist black blazer, Kam leaned back in her chair. "Whose accounts am I checking?"

"My father's."

"What?!" Kam hissed, leaning forward to fire questions. Eliza stopped her with a raised hand. "Can you do it?!"

"I-"

"Please Kam."

"To one Dr. Christine Daily, I show outlays in upwards of 50K." Kamari announced later, once her hacking expertise paid off. She'd gotten into Garrick Breck's business and personal accounts and quickly located the information his daughter wanted.

"50K-a lot of money," Kam noted, tapping her pen to the desk.

"He was in therapy-Simon was...for a while," Eliza shared while sitting on the opposite side of her desk. "Gambling."

Kam looked away from the monitor's flat screen. "What are you thinking?"

Eliza shook her head. "I don't know what to think."

"50K down the toilet is a helluva motive to hate."

"Hate enough to kill," Eliza supplied.

"El this is your dad we're talkin-"

"Jesus I know that Kam!"

"What can I do?"

"Go home," Eliza told her friend and stood to pace the office.

"Are you leaving too?" Kamari asked, moving from behind the desk.

"I'll be along."

"El-"

"Kam..." Eliza wasted no more time with words and came to clutch her friend's waist while leading her to the door. "I'll be fine. I'll think here better than at home okay?" she reasoned.

Kamari understood, especially since Eliza still lived with her parents. "Call me please."

Eliza pulled her into a tight hug. "Promise," she whispered, pressing a kiss to Kam's cheek.

***

Kamari went home and managed to shower and change clothes before worry set in more deeply than it had before she'd left Breck Tower. The doorbell rang just as she was about to put water on for tea. She was grateful for the interruption-until she saw who stood on the other side of her door.

"Came by the check on you," Huron explained, looking adorably uncertain as he stood in the hall with both hands hidden in the pockets of sagging black carpenter's jeans. "You left my office so upset."

Kam found herself stepping back in order to watch him more comfortably. "You always drop in to check on women who leave your office all emotional?" she tried to tease.

Huron shrugged beneath the whiskey brown cotton shirt that hung outside his jeans. "No. Only the tiny bow-legged ones."

Her mouth went dry and a sharp intake of breath drew Huron's jade stare to her chest. The black tank top she wore beneath a lightweight camouflage hoody, cupped her small yet full breasts in a manner that held his eyes captive.

"Come in," Kam said suddenly as if realizing she'd forgotten her manners.

"Come out with me," Huron asked instead. He didn't trust himself alone with her again. He might not be such a gentleman inside her apartment this time.

Kam slapped a hand to the side of the stylish camouflage Capris she sported. "I um…waiting on a call from Eliza," she said and glanced across her shoulder. "I can't go far…"

"Have you eaten?" he asked and leaned against the doorjamb.

"I was gonna make some tea."

The tiny admission curved Huron's mouth. "That's not food Kami."

She shrugged and leaned against the opposite side of the doorway. "I was thinkin' I might go down to the Café for a bite."

"Let's go," he said, pushing to his full height.

Nodding obediently, Kam was about to follow but he blocked her path.

"Keys? Cell?" He reminded.

"Right," she gushed, closing her eyes briefly to summon a few more ounces of brain power. She collected her things from the desk near the door and they set out.

"So tell me how a woman who looks as um…sweet as you gets herself involved in the ugly business of troubleshooting investigation?" Huron asked once they were settled into a booth with tea and water between them.

Kam smiled. "It's not always an ugly business," she clarified and took a sip of delicious blueberry green tea. "And has anyone ever accused you of being a sexist?"

"I'm sure someone has," he acknowledged, grimacing as he removed the lemon from his water glass, before taking a sip. "I've been called so much, it's hard to sort through it, you know?"

Kamari's laughter was only interrupted by the approach of their server. Once the young brunette had sauntered off with their orders for club sandwiches and fries, Huron fixed Kam with an expectant look.

"So? Let's hear it?" he prompted.

Averting her brown gaze, she smiled. "Why's it so important?"

"Because I want to know you."

Don't ask why, Kam ordered herself. "An accident really," she began and idly stirred the tea. "There was a company about to merge with the place I used to work for. Everybody was on edge about it-thinking we might lose our jobs, the new bosses might be jackasses, blah, blah, blah…I started doing some digging and came to the scary realization that uncovering dirt gave me a thrill."

Huron reared back on his side of the booth. He was thoroughly impressed by her honesty. "Was it good dirt?" he inquired.

Kam smirked. "If dirt had a rating system, this would be cream of the crop."

"Ha!"

"Precisely-on the top they were very glossy, respectable impressive list of charities which they gave an impressive amount of cash. They only failed to mention much of their cash was a result of vast holdings in pornography."

"You're kidding?" Huron accused, his glass posed mid-air.

Kam shook her head, sending a slew of curls into her face. "The employees were pretty pleased by it-you know...the possibility of naked staff meetings and such, of course."

"Of course," Huron took part in the teasing though his thoughts were wholly focused on the possibility of a naked meeting with his lovely dinner partner.

The conversation continued over delicious turkey clubs and seasoned fries. Through it all, Kam never realized how easy Huron was to talk to. Moreover, he was just as willing to answer her questions about his intriguing array of businesses.

"I know that during my investigation, I only found what you allowed me to find."

Huron grinned, but never looked away from the mustard he slathered on the last corner of his sandwich. "Shouldn't be so hard on yourself."

"Oh I'm not," she promised, her eyes locked on his powerful hands for a moment before she made herself look away. "I could've gone deeper if I needed to-besides, you'd gone to all that trouble."

"And you're certain you could've um...gone deeper?" He taunted, finally lifting his hypnotic greens to her face.

"Mmm..." Kam managed to gesture over the lump in her throat.

"So how much did you find?"

"Well once I discovered that you changed your name, the trail went dead."

"Hmph," he grunted, helping himself to a monster bite of the club.

"Which only leaves a new mystery."

Huron spared her a glance but looked back at his plate while he kept chewing. "And that would be?"

"Why?"

"Why'd I change my name."

"There's that. But I'd like to know why you changed it to Huron Base-gotta be a meaning there."

"Could be," he admitted and swallowed down a second glass of water. "That'd be for you to figure out-Miss Troubleshooting Investigator."

Kam raised her hands defensively. "Oh no, you're safe from me."

"You mean you don't want to go any deeper?"

Not if I plan to stay off my back, she supplied silently. She only graced Huron with a smile.

He tapped his fingers to the table and Kam felt that dangerous, yet scandalously delightful tingle. What was it about the man's hands? She wondered, believing she'd give anything to know what they'd feel like on her skin-what his fingers would feel like inside her body?

"There's got to be something more about me you want to know?"

Gasping, Kamari's wide eyes snapped to his face. "Honestly, I can't think of a thing," she lied and waved over the server to request more mayo for her sandwich.

Huron ceased his relentless teasing and the rest of the meal passed in easy silence.

***

After a week, Kamari felt more on edge than ever. Eliza hadn't contacted her once in spite of Kam's numerous voice and emails. She'd stopped herself from putting in an appearance at the Breck home or office. But Kam feared another day with no word might have her storming into the Breck domain and demanding answers.

On top of speculation and worry over her friend, there was the noticeable and mildly embarrassing state of her office. The place was starting to resemble a greenhouse. Plants of every variety had been arriving daily with cards from Huron Base that had Kam blushing and tingling interchangeably.

A few of the cards had found their way into the hands of various members of her staff which only increased Kam's embarrassment. Her employees couldn't have been more delighted to find their workaholic boss not knowing which way was up because of a man. The fact that he was gorgeous and sexy as sin simply compounded their glee. On Friday, her birthday, roses of every color arrived on the hour. Finally, she decided enough was enough-literally and paid a second visit to Huron's office.

***

Kamari wasn't surprised to find the assistant's desk vacant. Lord, didn't anyone ever work in this place? At his office door, she received a start when two well-dressed totem polls blocked the way. Kam swallowed her fear and prayed her voice wouldn't come out as a squeal when she introduced herself. Luckily, intros weren't necessary.

"Hell, B wasn't lyin' was he?" Rave Grant noted as he watched Kam approach.

"You surprised?" Nevil Willis cried softly as he also appraised Kam. "Damn fool can snap his fingers and have a dime honey pop out of thin air."

Kam managed a wavery smile when she stood before the towering men. "Good afternoon I'm-"

"Ms. Grade why don't you go on in and have a seat? He'll be done in a few." Nevil urged.

Kamari barely had time to be stunned that they knew who she was. Nevil and Rave left the room closing the door as they exited.

Huron's voice caught her ear as it always did and she turned. Seated in his preferred position, perched on the edge of his desk, he seemed to be ending a call. The only thing missing was the phone against his ear. Instead, he wore a headset, leaving his hands free to toss a baseball back and forth.

Kamari cleared her throat once he'd made plans to meet his phone partner for drinks and removed the headset. Huron turned. The closed expression he wore cleared immediately and was replaced by one of genuine delight.

"Happy Birthday Kami," he greeted softly and stood.

She opened her mouth and then closed it. Smiling, she acknowledged the greeting before dropping her wine-colored tote to a chair. "Huron what are you doing?"

"Being polite," he explained innocently, yet his striking stare glinted knowingly.

"The flowers?" she reminded, folding her arms across the front of the sleeveless V-neck shirt she wore.

"The flowers. Didn't you like them?" he asked, hunching over the desk to brace his hands atop it.

"They're filling my office-spilling over into my lobby and onto my employee's desks-what do you think?"

"Did that upset them?" he asked, appearing concerned.

"No. They love you for it. What are you doing?"

Hiding a hand in the pocket of his oatmeal heather trousers, he shrugged. "I thought maybe I was doing something nice for your birthday. Was I wrong?"

"Oh stop with the innocence," Kam ordered, tiring of playing the polite game. "You're no good at it."

Huron's heavy brows rose in a show of agreement. "So I've been told," he stepped around the desk. "You just strike me as the kind of woman who doesn't get flowers a lot-mostly because you're liable to threaten a guy's life if he sent them to you."

"And yet you sent them anyway," Kam noted, silently enjoying his impression of her.

Huron's steps slowed as he drew closer to her. "I like to live dangerously."

Kam couldn't hide her chuckle, especially since it felt so good to do so. In truth, Huron and the flowers had given her a much needed boost of escape from the drama with Eliza. Hearing the girl's name inside her head, drained Kam of whatever serenity she was experiencing then.

Huron noticed, his wicked grin vanished and concern crept into his eyes. Taking her wrist, he led her to one of the big chairs surrounding his desk. With a nudge, he made her sit.

"Tell me what's wrong."

"Eliza, I haven't heard from her." The words came out in a whisper.

"Were you expecting to?" Huron asked, his hand stroking her calf.

Kamari's lips thinned and she wouldn't respond. Huron didn't press. It didn't take much effort to figure it was something she wasn't sure she could trust him with. Giving her silence, he continued to kneel beside the chair and caress the bend of her knee.

Kamari recalled the last time she'd visited him there. He'd touched her as he did now. Like before, she was experiencing twin emotions of sensuality and comfort in spite of the fact that this time her legs were covered by black slacks. "Why are you doing this? Being so nice to me?" she added when he looked up.

"Aren't people usually nice to you?"

"Not people I've cut out of multimillion dollar deals."

Laughing fully now, he shook his head. "What can I say? I'm a glutton for punishment."

"So that's it?"

His humor disappeared instantly. "Jesus you can't be this dense?" he snapped, his hand firming behind her knee.

Before Kam knew what she was in for, his mouth was on hers. She could do nothing more than take and enjoy. Enjoying was certainly no great effort. His tongue stroked in much the same manner as his hand did her calf. These strokes to her mouth however were heated and lengthy and forced moans from the depths of her throat. Still kneeling before her, Huron parted her legs and settled himself neatly between.

Kam eagerly participated in the slow, exploring kiss. Smoothing her palms over his chest and linking her fingers behind his neck, she moved as close as the position would allow.

"That's it. That's *why*." He said, breaking the kiss to answer her question. His eyes were fierce as they bore deep into hers. "You terrify and arouse me equally and at the same time. A rush like that is hard to turn away from," he admitted.

"You're not a stupid man Huron," Kamari breathed, speaking as best she could while recuperating from his kiss. "You have to know this would never work."

"I disagree."

The simple words, voiced in a tone of finality brought a frown to Kam's brow. "Just like that?" she hissed, ignoring the intentionally lurid manner his incredible deep set gaze raked her body. "So what? You think something entitles you to have the last say?" she challenged, rolling her eyes when his brows lifted in confirmation.

The ring of her cell pierced the air and put Kam's thoughts back on her concerns.

"El?"

"No, no Kamari I'm sorry. This is Jessica Breck."

"Yes, yes ma'am." Kam whispered, feeling a foreboding chill. A call from her best friend's mother couldn't have been good news. Unconsciously, she clutched the lapel of Huron's suit coat.

"Sweetie forgive me for upsetting you, but Eliza-Eliza's in the hospital."

"Hosp-why? What happened to her?"

"Shh…she's alright," Jessica urged in the soothing tone patented by mothers. "She's fine. Are you able to come to the hospital love?"

"Yes," Kam gasped, nodding as Jessica gave the hospital name and Eliza's room number. "I'm on my way," she said, clicking off the phone as she stood. "I've got to go." She told Huron and patted his chest absently before she ran out the door.

***

"She confronted Gary about Simon. He'd always bailed that boy out of one mess or another. I don't care how many doctors Gary paid, Simon was never going to turn away from gambling. When his money ran out and his parent's cut him off…he found a way to get the money from the company."

Kamari stood in the hospital corridor rubbing her hands across her arms. She'd already guessed much of what Jessica Breck had just shared. "Why is she here?"

Jessica looked across her shoulder towards Eliza's room. "Gary...Gary admitted he killed Simon," she said in a tone of utter disbelief.

"Mrs. Breck? You want to sit down?" Kam urged, her eyes narrowed in concern.

Jessica shook her head. "I um, I guess he finally accepted that he couldn't save Simon-and please call me Jessica. You've been friends with my daughter for years."

Kam nodded. "Is that why El's here? She couldn't handle what her father told her?"

"Gary couldn't handle it-and he certainly couldn't handle Liza knowing." Jessica said, smoothing a hand across her blonde locks drawn back into a low ponytail. "They were very close and the scene between them turned ugly. Liza said she stormed out-went to her office and brooded a while. She was on her way back to apologize to her father and talk about what to do next when-she heard the shot. My husband's dead Kamari. Liza found her dad in his office where he'd killed himself."

Kam's eyes widened and blurred with tears. Both hands rose to cover her mouth and she shook her head. "Liza," she breathed.

"She thinks it's her fault. She passed out right in front of me after telling what happened."

"No, no it wasn't El's fault."

"None of that," Jessica ordered, turning to squeeze Kam's shoulder. "My daughter needs you and your strength. What happened between Garrick and Simon was inevitable. Simon had gone too far-too many times."

"I should see her."

Jessica nodded and patted Kamari's arm. "You do that. She's um...they've got her drugged, but she'll know you're there. I've got to get started on damage control," she squared her shoulders. "News about this'll be out soon. I'm grateful to you. Eliza's lucky to have you."

"Thank you Jessica."

Inside Eliza's room, Kam tried to tamp down her emotions. Taking a seat at the bedside, Kam pressed a kiss to Eliza's hand and kept hold of it. Softly, she whispered scolding words to her best friend. Words of apology and love followed and mingled with tears. She wouldn't let herself entertain more thoughts of how her profession played into what had happened. Eliza needed her and there was no time for wallowing in her own self pity.

An hour later, Kam left the room in hopes of scoring a cup of coffee. The corridor now teemed with executives and Breck family members, Kamari saw notepads in the hands of several so-called 'executives' and wondered how many were reporters trying to get the scoop on the latest Breck scandal.

She stopped and waited. Huron was there and Kam considered heading in the opposite direction. She couldn't move though. When he caught sight of her, she actually prayed he'd be kind.

Kamari wouldn't have worried. Immediately, he excused himself from the conversation he took part in. He said nothing when they stood face to face and simply opened his arms to her. Kam closed her eyes and fell against him as waves of tension melted away. Her tears fell heavy and were filled with a mix of grief over her friend, weariness and plain disgust.

"Shh...shh, love. It's alright. It's alright. Shh..." Huron urged, burying his face in her bright curls before lifting her close.

Kamari felt drained once the tears were spent. It was some time before she realized Huron was carrying her towards the elevators.

"Huron-"

"Goin' to your place. I want you to pack a few things and then it's off to parts unknown."

"But I can't-"

"No arguments."

"I can't just traipse off to *parts unknown* with you."

"Why not?" Huron asked, holding her contentedly while waiting for the elevator as though it were the most natural thing.

"I've got a business to run, other cases, people are depending on me..." she rambled, putting for the best argument a woman could while being nestled nice and neat in the arms of a gorgeous thing like Huron Base.

"Are you done?" he asked when she'd silenced to catch her breath.

Before she could decide, he was kissing her. The languid thrusts and rotation of his tongue was as mind-altering as usual. Wavery moans flooded Kamari's throat as she reciprocated the thrusts with her own brand of fire. Curling her fingers into the silky black of his hair, she arched into his chest and trailed her tongue along the even ridge of his teeth. Huron deepened the kiss even as the elevator doors parted and he stepped inside.

"I don't know you," she moaned when he finally released her mouth.

Grinning down, Huron leaned close to nudge her nose with his. "Mmm hmm and we're about to change that."

Book II

Layers of Deceit

LLL

Kamari Grade could hardly believe the sound of her own voice when she heard herself posing an argument *against* traipsing off to parts unknown with Huron Base. Yet, there she was, nestled in his incredible embrace and telling him she couldn't leave the hospital as Eliza might wake up needing her.

"You're an incredible friend," Huron was saying some ten minutes later when they were settled in a remote corner of a quiet waiting area.

Kam leaned forward, bracing elbows to knees while rubbing hands across her tired eyes. "I don't really have a choice- I could never see myself turning my back on her. Friendship is a thing she desperately needs."

Huron's striking greens narrowed then in curiosity. Kam smiled and offered a lazy shrug.

"Her family life...she needs friendship like a thirsting man needs water sometimes."

"I've always got the feeling that there's a lot of love between she and her parents."

Kam acknowledged Huron's soft observation with a rueful smirk. "That comes and goes. Especially when it comes to her mother."

"Jessica?"

"Mmm...the woman wanted to disown El after what happened with Cousteau. Cousteau Morgan." She clarified, having caught yet another of Huron's curious stares.

"The reporter?" He inquired.

Kam leaned back on the simply burgundy sofa that flanked the matching armchair Huron occupied. She wasn't all that surprised that he'd heard of the man. "He made quite a name for himself following that expose he did on the Brecks: *Success and Scandal*." She sighed, grimacing as a gust of cold air triggered gooseflesh along her bare arms. "I thought Jessica could've killed El when that story aired."

"That all must've been during my hermit stage. I never heard a thing about it." Huron was saying while he left the armchair to sit next to Kam on the sofa.

She settled happily into the crook of his arm when he pulled her close and rubbed her bare skin in a soothing fashion that supplied instant warmth. "The Breck lawyers did some fancy steppin' to pull it fast" She sighed again, eyes closing as the chill left her bones. "Trust me, if you've heard of Cousteau Morgan it's because of the Brecks."

"No Kami, I've heard of Cousteau Morgan because he used to work for me."

Kamari sat perfectly straight and speechless while Huron explained giving Cousteau his first 'big break'.

"Everybody thought I was crazy givin' the guy a shot as heard of a TV station." Huron grinned nudging his thumb against the dimple in his chin. He shrugged. "Hell, I'd only bought the place. Cous knew way more about runnin' it than I did so..."

It felt too good to laugh and Kam couldn't help but do so just then. "So what happened?" She was finally able to inquire further. "Cousteau wasn't working for you when he broke that story, was he?"

Huron winced, stroking the sleek whiskers smattering the curve of his jaw. "Cous always wanted to be in the grit." The memory made him grin briefly. "It was like a drug for him- out there digging for a story- not sittin' clean and pretty behind a desk being some TV bigshot." He shrugged and slanted Kam an easy look. "That was ten years ago. The station's still makin' money hand over fist. I told him he's always got a job there if he wants it."

"You speak with him on the regular?" Kam sat up a little straighter on the couch.

"No. Why?"

"I know El misses him." Kam's light stare was focused across the room. "She never really went into all of what happened- all she kept saying during that time was that her loyalty was to her parents."

Huron didn't like the darkening of Kamari's expression one bit. Before he had the chance to probe deeper, a nurse was calling to Kam from the doorway of the waiting room.

"She's asking for you Ms. Grade."

Huron caught Kam's hand before she bolted from the sofa. "Dinner later?"

Kam was already shaking her head. "El, I have to-"

"You've got to eat," he argued giving her hand a small shake. "I'll be back in an hour or so. I'll take you to eat-"

"Huron I-"

"And I'll bring you back here to spend the night if you like."

Kamari relaxed a little with that final statement. She was sure his plans had involved her spending the night with him. She'd be first to admit that she was being tremendously silly, but she was already dangerously attracted to the man. Alone time with him would only lead to one place- and heaven help her that was a place she was growing more and more curious about.

"Sound good?" He stood, tilting his head a tad while waiting for her response.

"I-yes- yes, it sounds good."

"What are you afraid of Kami?" His hand smothered both of hers then.

"Mixing pleasure with my business," she blurted in a breathy, defeated tone. "It's sure to involved you again at some point. I know it."

Huron smiled glancing toward her hands in his and looking every bit like he'd come to the same conclusion. "Does it have to be a problem?" His gaze was still on their hands.

"You have to know it will be." She waited for his eyes to meet hers, and then left him with a sorrowful smile and exited the room.

***

Jessica Breck was going through papers on her late husband's desk- trying to decide what to keep, handle or toss...or at least that's what she *hoped* it looked like she was doing. A firm, single knock to the open office door interrupted her task. Guarded intensity crept into her blue eyes when she spotted her brother in law Samuel standing there.

"What are you doing here?" She silently cursed the stunned quality of her voice. She'd bet anything he'd been standing there just watching her long before he decided to knock.

"Just observing." He pushed off the doorjamb, glancing around his deceased brother's office with just the hint of a smile curving his mouth. "You look comfortable Jess."

She bristled but refused to bite just then. "Business goes on. There's bound to be things here needing to be handled." She waved her hand once over the unkempt desk. "In a situation like this, the first thing people will expect is for business to slip and we certainly can't afford that."

"Hmph," Sam smirked and glanced around the office again. "Sounds good Jess- real good."

"Dammit Sam, exactly what are you trying to imply? Surely not that I'm happy my husband is dead?"

"Of course not," Sam's expression lost its teasing hue. "You loved my brother, I know that. But you can't deny him never giving you a firm place in the company was a source of tension between the two of you." He folded his arms across the worsted gray suitcoat buttoned over the crisp black shirt and tie beneath it. "With Gary gone you can *slip in* now so to speak."

Jessica's lashes fluttered in the midst of her temper arching. "I'd appreciate you leaving."

"What I can't figure," Sam contined as if he hadn't heard the request, "is why Gary would kill Simon when they'd always been so close." He shrugged. "Closer than I would've liked at times…Gary had to know I'd never approve of him giving Simon that sort of money."

It was Jessica's turn to shrug. "Everyone gets tired of being an ATM Sam."

Sam seemed to consider the flip statement, and then smiled. "Don't work too hard Jess."

Alone, Jessica made a pretense at shuffling a heap of papers. Moments later she dropped the act and slumped back into her husband's desk chair.

***

When Huron returned to collect Kamari for their dinner date, he was of course greeted most eagerly by every nurse at the station. They said they hoped he was there to pull Kam off her post. Some were bold enough to add that she'd be a fool to refuse leaving with him.

Huron accepted the flattery and flirtation graciously and without conceit. Not surprising when such things occurred in his world on an almost daily basis. He asked the nurses if Kam was still with Eliza and was told she'd been asleep for the past half hour.

Huron didn't know whether to feel relief or agitation when he found her slumped over a chair next to Eliza's bed. Closing the door without so much as a click of the lock, he strolled over on silent footsteps and took a few moments to study her. Gradually, his thoughts returned to his actions over the last few weeks. Never had a woman instilled such a reaction in him. Sure there was sexual attraction- *was there ever*- but never a desire- a need to enfold and protect.

Gently, he trailed fingers through her bright crop of hair. This unsuspectingly dynamic woman was fast becoming a beacon that he craved in the darkness that was his life. His fingers drifted away as her earlier words that afternoon echoed in his head. Her cautions against mixing pleasure and her business…Couldn't he have boasted the same caution? Like the infamous Brecks, his business was also a story of success rooted in much scandal. So much so, he wondered whether she could overlook it. Moreover, would *he* want her to?

Eliza stirred, her eyes opening as she did so. "Huron?" She whispered once her blurred gaze had focused.

"How are you?" He left Kam to smile down at her friend.

"I'll be much better once they let me out of here." She smiled a bit before her gaze clouded.

"I'm sorry about your father. He was a good man." Huron read the sadness in her expression.

Eliza's 'thank you' was barely audible. She took a breath as though attempting to clear her mind and looked over at her sleeping friend.

"Get her out of here, would you?" She asked Huron while smiling apologetically at Kam. "She's spending too much time at my bedside. She's concerned for me, but I know it's more about guilt. She thinks her work…what she discovered, caused this somehow. It's unfounded."

Fully agreeing, Huron nodded. "I won't be able to keep her away for long." He warned, brushing the back of his hand across Kam's cheek. "I do intend to see she gets a good meal, though."

El nodded enthusiastically against her pillow. "That's a good start."

Kam didn't awaken until they were in the elevator where a strange sense of déjà vu washed over her.

"Not quite," Huron said when she shared her feelings. "This time we're actually getting out of this place."

Instead of feeling on edge upon realizing she was in his arms again, Kamari felt strangely content. She glanced up, noticed his striking greens focused and unflinching on her face and she offered a weak smile.

"Don't hurt me for this, alright?" He pleaded, holding onto her as though there were nothing out of the ordinary about her being there nestled in his arms. "I got Eliza's full permission to get you out of here."

"And I'm way too tired to argue, but I can't let you carry me all the way out of here."

His fingers flexed a tad where they clutched her thigh. "Just exactly how do you propose to stop me?"

Kam bit her lip, never realizing how enticing an image she cast upon the man carrying her. "What exactly would you require?" She asked.

"Are you sure you'd like to know?"

Her eyes settled to the sultry curve of his mouth. "I think I can guess."

Barely had the words left her lips than his head dipped and they were kissing. The act was a mixture of tenderness and heat. Wavering moans resonated deep in Kam's throat while she arched closer seeing- craving the thrust and rotation between his tongue and hers.

When the elevator reached their destination, walking on her own accord was the last thing on Kam's mind. She gave silent thanks that the elevator trip was an uninterrupted one and had to question her actions as of late. Never in a million would she believe she'd ever be caught in an elevator kissing the bejesus out of a man while he carried her!

"Another limo." She regained the use of her verbal skills to scold him when they approached the waiting car parked a few feet from the elevator area.

Huron gave a one-shoulder shrug. "Would you believe I hardly use the thing?"This time, he was the one biting his lip on uncertainty. "It's only in service when I meet with someone I need to speak with seriously during a drive."

Kam offered a smile to the driver who held open the door while Huron deposited her in the lush dark interior of the car. Her cheeks burned with embarrassment but she ordered herself to move past it. Chances were, such situations would be frequent while she was in the presence of Huron Base.

"So are we going to...talk seriously?" She asked once they were settled and the car was headed from the parking deck.

"We could talk too."

"This will be a mistake." She dismissed the suggestion behind his reply.

For the first time since he'd known her, the stirrings of frustration began to nudge Huron's admirably controlled temper. "Jesus I wish you'd stop telling me that." He massaged his eyes and leaned forward a tad.

Kam wasn't put off by the edge to his low voice. "In my business it helps to be up front."

"Well your business sucks."

"Very much at times, but it is what it is." She smiled and was quite close to laughter.

"Well then, in that case I'll play fair and be up front too." He angled his frame with the ease of a big cat. "I want you in bed- any bed will do. I won't deny that I think of it often." He smirked at the widening of her vibrant stare. "I also won't deny that I want much more- though I'm not altogether sure what that is. Anyway, it's only right that you know when I'm intent on having something, I employ every means at my disposal to get it." He cast a fleeting glance in the direction of her bosom which heaved excessively in the wake of her surprise.

Kamari couldn't help but to allow the comment to slide without argument. The remainder of the drive passed in silence.

"This isn't a good idea." Kam didn't care how much like a broken record she sounded.

Huron's home was nestled in the remote picturesque domain of Marin County- the gateway to wine country.

"I...I can't stay too long...Eliza," she muttered gaze still focused on the beauty spread out before her.

"She wants her hospital room to herself for a while so I'm afraid you've got no where to go. Eliza told me so herself," he added feeling Kam's stunned gaze boring holes into him.

"What are we gonna do out here?" Kam spoke the first words that came to mind when he slammed the limo door shut.

Huron crowded her near the car- easy to do considering his wide towering frame. "I've only got dinner in mind, but always open to suggestion."

She would've surely given in to the weakening of her legs then had he not chosen that moment to ease an arm about her waist and escort her toward the house.

Kam felt like a virgin being led to her deflowering and would've laughed over the comparison had she not been so in awe of his home. She'd expected it to be grande. No one lived as roughly as he had and not chosen to surround himself with the best once he was able to do so.

Still, she hadn't expected such warmth to be part of it. Like a snug blanket it enfolded her and relaxation beckoned instantly.

"Do you like it?" Huron surprised himself by asking not realizing how eagerly he anticipated her response- her approval.

Kam of course was full of accolades and lavished them generously. "I can't believe it looks so lived in," she blurted and heard his intake of breath. She was stunned and a great deal amused to find that the well meaning comment had bruised his ego.

"It's obvious and impressive that you spend lots of time at home." She carefully rephrased. "I expected you to be a man who only kept a home so the post office would have somewhere to deliver your mail."

He laughed then- full, hearty and ego forgotten. "That's actually not far from the truth." He looked around then too in clear approval of his home. "I spend lots of time away but when I come home, I expect to be comfortable and this place hasn't let me down yet."

They continued the tour with it ending perfectly in the den where drinks and appetizers waited. Kam noted how precisely he'd planned for a simple dinner.

"Nothing about you is simple so why should dinner be any different?" He posed the challenging question while helping himself to one of the cream cheese filled pin-wheels.

Meanwhile, Kamari strolled the room observing that it was littered with tiny clues to his past. Framed pictures of all sizes revealed that he wasn't the loner she'd suspected. There were shots of a younger Huron Base with a lovely woman whose eyes bore a striking resemblance to his own. There were others with various young men and an even younger Huron in a baseball uniform. Kam eased back from the photos, suddenly feeling as if she were prying-viewing too much.

"Why'd you bring me here?" She could feel him watching her from his place near the serving table.

"You're a smart woman." Huron didn't pretend to misunderstand and helped himself to another pinwheel. "Please don't tell me again why this is a mistake." With his free hand, he poured a glass of wine and carried it over to her. His smile was grim as he watched her drink deeply from the hefty goblet. He took it before she could drain the contents.

"Hey-"

"You need to eat."

"Exactly why are you going to all this trouble with me?" The bit of wine she'd downed loosened her tongue enough to ask the question she'd been wracking her brain trying to find an answer to.

He grinned and had the nerve to grace her with a wink. "It's no trouble at all Kam."

"Please- my job- sorry," she raised a hand in defense when his expression darkened. "But seriously, it *is* an issue- as are my obligations to my best friend..." she smoothed her hands across her bare arms and cast a look around the room. "Forgive me but I'm sure you rarely if ever have to go to such lengths to tug a woman into your bed. Hell," she laughed, "I'm sure *tug* is even too strong of a word. Most women probably just *glide* between your sheets."

"Wow...thanks for the compliment." He chuckled and finished off the rest of her wine. "Your opinion of me remains high in spite of all you know about my colorful past."

"But I don't know anything about you." Her voice was syrupy sweet.

"Then isn't dinner the perfect way to change that?"

She chose not to respond and Huron was glad since he had a fine idea of what she'd say. He could almost see her battling with herself- desperately trying to create more and more reasons against letting anything more involved grow between them.

"Are you afraid of me Kamari?" He could no longer suppress the need to ask.

Kam blinked and somehow managed to keep her gaze focused on his. She couldn't answer and it wasn't because the answer was yes. She wasn't afraid of him. In spite of his reputation and what she knew of his past, she sensed a goodness in him.

It was the unknown that unsettled her. What she didn't know about him- what she'd been unable to uncover about him had begun to gnaw at her more steadily the longer she knew him. What secrets of his past would she discover if he chose to allow those layers to be peeled away? Could she handle it all? Or would she run hysterical and terrified over the man he was...the man he'd been?

They blinked simultaneously as if discovering they were no longer alone in the den. Dinner was being announced. Huron was grateful for the interruption. He didn't want to acknowledge the fact that she hadn't- *couldn't* answer him. While she hadn't exactly admitted fear, she hadn't exactly denied it.

Without a word, he raised a hand to beckon her to him and out of the room. When she moved past him and his nostrils flared at the drift of her perfume, he called himself a fool. What should he have expected? Any woman in her right mind would be uneasy as hell over being with him.

Though he'd found more than a few who got off on the idea of danger and dangerous men, few understood what a truly dangerous man was all about. When one stripped away the layer of glamour; which added a certain sex appeal to the label, and revealed the purely *unsexy* ugliness, *that* was the real face of it. Few women had the guts, nerve...or indecency to stick around.

Kamari maintained her silence during the trip to the dining room. She knew her silence had hurt him and she regretted it for he'd shown her nothing but kindness. Still, he'd asked, hadn't he? Yes, he'd asked and she hadn't the good grace to answer. Whatever she might find in the future regarding his past, it would never diminish the fact that she wanted him. She wanted to know what he'd feel like against her...inside her...

"Kam?" He smiled apologetically when she jumped at the sound of his voice.

Kamari realized she'd stopped dead in her tracks when her thoughts took over. "Sorry," she muttered, glancing in his direction but not making eye contact. She headed in the direction he motioned.

***

Malibu, California~

Cousteau Morgan grimaced as the third shot of Irish Whiskey burned its path down his gullet. As he'd just finished off a half bottle of Bourbon, he thought the whiskey would be a nice mellow companion to his journey toward drunkenness. He should know the Irish never did anything mellow.

His vivid turquoise stare shifted towards the accordion folder lying a few inches away. Some of its holdings were just visible and spilling out of the folder's wide mouth. Cousteau blinked away as if the action would hide what those holdings revealed.

No good. He'd read and re-read again once the material had been forwarded. He'd always felt there was more to uncover, but even he; with his deep well of journalist's cynicism, never expected anything like this.

What to do with it, was the question now. Perhaps nothing. Cousteau smirked, revealing a left dimple that seemed to splice his cheek in a sinfully appealing way. Yeah, doing nothing always sounded good- at least to him. Why stop now? Especially when doing nothing had cost him Eliza. Not much had mattered since he let that happen anyway, so why stop now?

But he hadn't stopped, had he? He'd gone right ahead and dug until he'd dug up the real stink of it and boyo did it stink. It stunk to high heaven. He'd come there to his place in Malibu. It was the one eccentricity he'd allowed himself during those happy money days working for Huron Base.

He'd come there to plot his next move. Nothing…yeah, nothing always sounded good.

**

"This was an incredible meal Huron. Thank you." Kam couldn't resist raving over the dinner in spite of the fact that the event itself had been tense-filled and quiet.

The quiet however had allowed them both to enjoy the wonderful spread of Salmon patties, steamed veggies on a bed of brown rice, a wheat bread that had to be fresh from the oven. It smelled like heaven.

"Thanks Kam." Huron seemed pleased by her approval of the food. The smile curving his mouth though appeared a little less than easy. "Are you done?" He asked.

Kam only nodded while accepting that the dark cloud hanging over their evening would remain. Quietly, they left the dining room. Kam was about to ask whether they should at least clear the table when she noticed a uniformed man emerge from a concealed entryway to handle the chore.

She felt Huron's hand at the small of her back, pressing lightly but with an underlying possessiveness. Swallowing over a moan, she let him guide her through the dim corridor which took them back to the den.

Kam blinked several times in response to the room's mild transformation. Gone was the platter of appetizers and bucket of wine. All artificial lighting had been shut down and the area was lit by the snapping flames in the fireplace. Kam had almost forgotten how chilly that neck of the woods could be especially when one lived so close to the water. She welcomed the warmth of the fire but had little time to dwell on its comfort. She was affected by an entirely different source of heat when Huron took hold of her arm.

In one seamless motion he turned her and took her mouth with his tongue in virtually the same movement. Kam could do nothing to stifle the whimper that soared past her throat. She felt as though she were being consumed by the licking flames of the fire. She melted. Her next moan weakened her lips and afforded Huron more room to explore. Her fingers clenched and unclenched within the material of the wood grain shirt that hung outside his loose-fitting dark trousers.

Kamari felt herself moving or being moved backward and dismissed from her mind any concerns about where he was guiding her. Huron's kiss demanded nothing less than all of her attention. Kam wanted nothing more than to give it to him.

His hold upon her arms firmed and Kam knew she was being lifted, drawn closer to him. She didn't want to open her eyes afraid the magic would end, that reality would set in with all its harshness.

There was suddenly the wondrous feel of soft, firm cushioning beneath her body- the sofa. Huron broke the kiss then, trailing his persuasive mouth across Kam's cheek and along the sensitized spot below her ear. She heard him say her name and felt the word vibrate through his massive chest. She bit down on her lip when his hands roamed her hips; curving beneath her ample buttocks and easing her into him. Her eyes opened wide at the sensation of his arousal next to hers.

Absently, she pressed on his chest-not really meaning for him to stop but feeling as though she should initiate some form of protest. The action however did nothing to stop her from seeking his mouth with hers and instigating her own kiss.

Huron heard what sounded like a whimper rise from *his* chest and knew then that *he* was seconds away from calling a halt to the scene. He'd never whimpered a day in his life and wouldn't even admit to the gesture when he was a child. Yet in his heart he knew the sound came from him. This woman appealed to him on every level. As powerfully as he'd denied having even uttered a whimper, he just as powerfully denied having ever felt quite so terrified.

Once again; in his heart, he knew that's exactly what he was- terrified.

Faintly, Kam heard chimes and it eventually registered that her phone alarm was going off. She recalled setting it earlier to sound in a few hours. As she believed the evening would possibly culminate with her in Huron's bed, she sought to do whatever she could to prevent it.

"What the hell is that?" Huron growled amidst the ravishing thrusts of his tongue against hers as he tuned in to the delicate chiming.

Feeling utterly foolish then, Kam awkwardly reached into her trouser pocket to shut down the alarm. "I um...I set it so I wouldn't be away from El too long." Her explanation sounded hushed, embarrassed as she was. Huron bowed his head but not before she glimpsed the muscle flexing in his cheek when his jaw tightened. For several moments, she was captivated by the harsh beauty of his face.

"I should be getting back." She managed when his emerald greens shifted to meet her gaze.

Huron felt his jaw beginning to ache, he'd clenched it so tight. Unfortunately, he feared his mounting frustration would get the better of him if he loosened up to speak. He allowed himself a second or two longer not ready to relinquish the feel of her pliant beneath him. Her small plump bosom heaving against his chest was simply an agitating reminder that he'd not indulged in the taste and texture of her nipples on his tongue. The thought roused another whimper and gingerly he pushed off her.

Kam couldn't move once his weight left her. She actually felt bereft-like a part of her was missing. Quickly she dismissed the idea. She hadn't known Huron Base long enough to feel such a connection, had she?

Huron was turned away while he rooted around his pockets for keys. "Get your stuff. I'll take you back."

Kam blinked out of her thoughts for the second time that night. The tone of finality in his words told her she'd probably aggravated him enough that time for him to finally be done with whatever he'd thought of starting with her. She left the big sofa fixing her clothes, grabbed her bag from an armchair and followed him from the room.

***

"So are you afraid to admit it? Even to yourself?"

"No. Because there's nothing to admit."

"Mmm...I'm pretty sure Huron doesn't think so."

Kam rolled her eyes while dragging all ten fingers through the disarray of her auburn curls. "I'm pretty sure you've got some packing to do since you're getting out of here today."

Eliza remained where she was, seated in the middle of the bed with her knees drawn up to her chin. "I've been packed since they gave me my release date." Her response was as smug as the smile she wore.

It was a week later and El's doctor was finally in agreement that she could complete the rest of her recuperation at home.

"So are you afraid to admit it to yourself?" El persisted.

Kam slumped down in the bedside chair she'd occupied. "It'd be a mistake...eventually. Why go into it knowing it'll end badly?"

"Because he's Huron Base?" El's arched brows rose in a dreamy manner while her shoulders rose to nudge the glossy blonde waves of her hair. "Because he's irresistible and incredible looking?" She grew serious then. "And because I think it all goes way deeper than looks."

Kam's laughter filled the room. "And how do you know this?"

"Ah Kam, please stop pretending that you don't understand." Eliza smacked a fist to her palm. "There's something intense and dangerous mixed in with something thoughtful and gentle. All that rolled together is a recipe for sexiness." She waved her hands to keep Kam from interrupting.

"All I'm saying is maybe you should chance it- you know you'll wonder over it forever if you don't."

Again, Kam laughed and leaned over to hit the toe of Eliza's sneaker-shod foot. "You've been cooped up in here too long with all your tear jerker movies and romance novels." She leaned back in the chair, refusing to acknowledge the part of her that was in full agreement.

Eliza's doctor and nurse entered the room then. The doctor carried release papers for signing and a few final instructions for his patient. Eliza was so happy to be released she didn't even argue about the wheelchair and sat down eagerly with a smile.

"I'm taking the longest soak in the history of soaks and sleeping naked in my own bed for at least the next two days!" Eliza enthusiastically vowed once Kam was pushing her chair toward the elevators.

The rumble of a throat being cleared sounded nearby. Both women looked round to see Cousteau Morgan standing there.

Eliza swallowed, dared not blink and reached behind to grab Kamari's pant leg. Finally, her expressive blue gaze began to roam Cousteau's six foot plus frame, stopping repeatedly on his devastating face.

"Elly," he said, his own vivid stare observing her just as closely before he smiled and nodded toward Kamari. "How are you Kam?"

She nodded. "It's been a long time, Cousteau."

"What are you doing here?" Eliza blurted.

"I heard about Simon...."

The lilt of his baritone tinged with a hint of the Bronx caused Eliza to swallow over the sudden lump in her throat.

"and your father," he continued, habitually reaching up to smooth back fallen tendrils of wavy brown from his forehead. "I know you took it hard." He moved progressively closer as he spoke.

Eliza appeared dumbfounded. "How?"

"You forget we know many of the same people." A knowing smile sparked the lone dimple.

The slight reference to their former relationship, sent Eliza's cheeks to burning and her grip slackened on Kam's pant leg. Suddenly, she cleared her throat and forced a stern tint to her gaze. "I appreciate your condolences but I'm fine and on my way home so if you'll excuse us-"

"May I talk to you Elly?"

Her attempt at being stern oozed away. "Cousteau..."

"Please Elly?"

"I can't." She gave a decisive shake of her head and missed the way Cousteau's turquoise stare followed the swish of her hair.

"They've released me...might think I'm bent on staying if they see me hanging around."

"I could take you home." The suggestion was soft as he moved closer. "It's important and I've waited too long to let this slide any longer. Elly, please?"

"Shit." Eliza bowed her head to hiss the curse. "Kam... I'll uh...I'll see you later, okay?"

Kamari snapped to and knelt beside her friend's chair. "Are you sure?"

El was already nodding solemnly. "Guess I should take the advise I gave you a little while ago." She patted against the sleeve of Kam's hoody and smiled. "Go on I'll be fine-you get some rest, alright?"

Nodding eventually, Kam smoothed a hand across the black yoga pants covering Eliza's thigh. She stood then and left Cousteau with a nod.

***

While Kamari may've been reluctant to take Eliza's advice about Huron Base, she needed no further encouragement to take the advice about resting. She left the hospital and headed for home. There, she dumped her clothes into the hamper and spent the next twenty minutes in the shower. The hot water and luxurious liquid soap she'd selected, pampered her skin and mind in unison. Afterwards, she slipped into the first T-shirt she could find and poured herself into bed.

Kam woke hours later. She felt rested but still craved a few hours more sleep. It took a few seconds to blame her waking on the ringing phone.

"Mmm?" She grunted, having finally managed to grab the receiver. "Yes?" She greeted when the caller offered no response to her grunt.

"Kami? It's Huron."

The announcement pulled her promptly out of sleep mode. "Huron." She eased up to sit amidst the tangled covers. "How are you?" she inquired while grimacing over not coming up with a better question.

Obviously, Huron thought it was appropriate. "Not so good," he admitted. "I don't like the way things ended after our dinner. I'm sorry."

Kam winced as guilt stabbed at her. "I certainly played my part in how badly things ended, you know?"

"Can I see you?"

Her breath caught on the word 'yes'.

"Kam?"

"When?"

"Answer your doorbell."

Before she could tell him that it wasn't ringing, the phone connection broke. Suspicious then, she left the bed and stepped gingerly through her condo. At the door, she stood on her toes and peeked through the tiny privacy window. Smirking, she glanced down at the T-shirt which hardly covered her ass. The bell rang and she opened the door.

Huron gave himself a mental pat on the back for having perfect timing. He masked nothing in his jade stare while raking Kam's tiny frame encased beneath the barely there T-shirt.

Clearly embarrassed, Kam cast another critical look at her attire. "I wasn't expecting company."

"Am I interrupting?" He asked having sobered and believing he'd actually been holding his breath until she told him she'd been taking a nap.

"Is it a bad time?" He made himself ask though he had no intention of leaving as long as she was in that damn T-shirt.

Kam shook her head. She was as starved for his company as he was for hers. Stepping away from the door, she silently urged him inside and relished the chance to breathe in the now familiar scent of his cologne.

"I'll go change." She said while closing the door. When she turned, he was right there- crowding, towering... The dull, distracting throb that plagued her whenever she saw him was now threatening to buckle her knees.

Kam was on her toes again, this time arching up for his kiss before he'd even dipped his head. She bit her bottom lip and fixed him with an innocently expectant look when it appeared she'd assumed too much.

The affect on Huron was explosive. His mouth was fused upon hers mere seconds later. He pressed her back against the door, keeping her there while his tongue raked her teeth and explored the deepest recesses of her mouth. He caught her waist, lifting her slightly to accommodate their differing heights.

Kam eased her arms neatly about his neck and played in his soft hair for a time. Her nails raked the whiskers that offered light shadow to his fair skin.

He wouldn't fall in love with her, Huron assured himself. He'd never allow himself that weakness, he chanted the words inside his head while massaging her hips and back still covered by the T-shirt. He added more pressure to the kiss, his tongue plundering mercilessly as a voice chanted back that falling in love with her had already occurred.

Kamari felt her heart fly to her throat when Huron set her to her feet and tugged the shirt above her head. She hadn't bothered to put anything on underneath. For a second or three she was completely on edge about being bared to the man's striking stare. Huron set her away, indulging in several moments of sight seeing. He began a journey of touch, trailing his fingers down the line of her neck, across her collarbone, between the cleft of her breasts...

She was thankful for the door at her back and let her head rest against it. Her lashes fluttered down over her eyes like hummingbird wings when his fingers grazed her belly and past it. She heard him murmur something about wanting to know if her auburn hair was natural. He must have realized the information would be difficult to obtain as he brushed his thumb across the bikini-waxed area above her sex.

He got past his disappointment quickly of course and his fingers began an intense exploration of what lay beyond. Kamari's gasps filled the entryway of her condo when she felt his fingers plundering her body. Huron cursed when moisture covered his fingertips milliseconds after they'd disappeared inside her.

Kam held onto the doorknob for support and arched into the delicious caress. When his ring and index fingers joined the middle she rode them with a shameless eagerness.

"No please," she begged when he sought to end the orgasm-inducing fingering. She went as far as to grasp his wrist and draw him back.

Instead, Huron turned the tables and swung her high against his broad chest. Another kiss followed and Kam was once again an eager participant. Meanwhile, Huron was going through the condo interrmittedly breaking the kiss as he opened the doors with the tip of his boot in search of her bedroom.

Before Kam could give him directions, Huron was kissing her again and stifling any verbal communications. At last found the double doors at the end of the long corridor and her bedroom behind them.

Kam expected to be tossed down to the bed while he did her the great pleasure of letting her watch him take off his clothes. Huron had other plans and kept hold of her while following her down to the tangled bed. The kiss seemed to intensify and she felt her heart race with a new fire in response to the underlying determination she could feel radiating from him like a living thing.

Huron parted her legs; which quivered pitifully, and settled himself between. Kamari tried to pull the sport jacket from his shoulders when he broke the kiss to attend to her breasts. Intent on remaining clothed, he captured her wrists and linked five fingers through all ten of hers while keeping her hands above her head. The movement raised her firm breasts a bit higher and he snuggled down in comfort to suckle a firm nipple while manipulating its twin with his free hand.

Indecipherable sounds rose from Kam's throat. She bit her lip while grinding herself against the sweetly stiff length of his arousal straining against the zipper of his jeans. He'd ravaged her nipples well beyond the point when they'd grown erect and glistening from the favors of his lips and tongue.

"More," she ordered surprising herself and Huron. She was far too overwhelmed to care.

Grinning devilishly, he obeyed freeing her hands to outline her breasts with the tip of his tongue before the organ grazed downward across the plane of her tummy and the bare patch of skin he'd lightly explored earlier.

A wavering 'yes' floated from Kam's mouth when his tongue thrust deep inside her core moments later. She raked her fingers through the crisp dark curls covering his head which nudged her palms during his ravenous feasting upon her body.

Her thighs shook madly until he caught them, forcing them to still. Kam was torn between delight and torture. Her body writhed and trembled upon the covers, loving the deep strokes of his tongue but needing more…much more. She pleaded with him again but he wouldn't oblige until she was totally clear about what she wanted.

"You. *This.*" She ground herself against the erection beneath his jeans when he rose above her. "I want this inside me. Please Huron...please..."

No room left for misunderstanding then, Huron lost a bit more of his strength. His head fell to her shoulder. There, he took many deep breaths.

Kam thought she'd said something wrong for he lay there still as a board but for the flexing of his fingers on her hips. She felt his weight leave her and looked to his face for some sign of disapproval.

Instead, she noticed the devilish grin had reappeared along with something unrecognizable but utterly alluring in his emerald eyes. Kam swallowed at the feel of her heart still residing in her throat when he pulled the mocha sport jacket from his back. It was followed in rapid succession by the black crewneck, boots and jeans. His need was evident beneath the boxers and Kam moaned when he stepped close to allow her fingers to explore the rigid pack of abs, past the waistband of his underwear...with a slight tug, she quietly ordered them gone and he obliged.

Huron whispered a hushed obscenity when their nude bodies met in the center of the bed. Kam could only murmur unintelligible remarks as she wriggled to accommodate his frame between her thighs.

His body was poised to enter hers when memory surged and his head fell to her chest.

"Huron?" She whispered, locking her legs about his waist when he moved to go. "No way are you leaving me now." She told him humorlessly.

There was no devilish intent in Huron's smile that time. There was only possessiveness and a fair amount of captivation. Faintly, he recalled his decision on not falling in love with her- not wanting to succumb to that weakness.

The weakness however was something he was beginning to crave like a drug. He'd spent longer than he cared to remember being strong, overbearing, intimidating...deadly. He knew weakness was dangerous. He never realized it could be like a soothing oasis- that it could be like home.

"Huron?" Concern filtered Kam's lush brown stare then.

Leaning close, he kissed the corner of her mouth. "I'm only getting condoms from my jacket."

Kam winced, berating herself for being so far gone to not remember that very important item. "You came prepared," she relaxed her legs around his waist.

"Hopefully," he corrected in a purely honest fashion.

Kamari closed her eyes when he moved away and willed her heart to remain immune to the man.

Huron retrieved the condoms and; once protection was handled, he settled back to the place that had become his favorite spot. Indulging in a deep kiss that had them both panting, each sought to drink in the essence of the other.

Kam was so caught up in the throaty kiss, that his erection inside her body brought her quickly to orgasm. She moaned the word 'no' as emotion seized her.

Huron gave no quarter as he took her relentlessly and unmindful of her pleading with him to give her a minute. Kam was caught between pitting her strength against his chest and praying that she was multi-orgasmic. She smiled, realizing that it had never mattered before.

Tiring of her fists on his chest, Huron captured her wrists and once again positioned them above her head. Kam cheered her body's cooperation as she came down off the climax only to feel the sensations back-building.

Huron was focused again on her nipples, this time barely nibbling upon them with his perfect lips and teeth. That, combined with the wide, lengthy thrusts of his sex inside the drenched deep cavern of her own brought orgasm two just as quickly.

As his ego was being as thoroughly stroked as the rest of him, something else was at work there. Without him even being aware of it happening at first, Kam had brought to life something he didn't know existed within him. She'd appealed to the part of his manhood that wanted to cherish, protect... love?

God there was so much she didn't know about him- so much they didn't know about each other. This had happened very quickly even by *his* standards. Quick or not, the lovely Ms. Kamari Grade had undoubtedly sealed her fate. She was his and whether he admitted it or not, he was hers.

***

Eliza stifled the tempting swell of laughter creeping up her throat over the memory which had just struck her. God, the things one remembered when under stress, she thought. No man, not even her father or other male relatives had been inside her apartment since the night she ordered Cousteau Morgan out of it over two years ago. Now, he was back. She prayed he'd say what he had to and leave, knowing she'd die all over again if he left her twice in a lifetime.

"Would you like to take your bath first?" He asked once they stood facing each other awkwardly across her living room.

Eliza felt the laughing sensation continue its journey up the back of her throat. Smothering it, she put cool indifference in its place. "Get to the point. What's so important you had to bring me back here to say it?"

"You never let me finish what I had to tell you the night you told me to go." His voice was soft. He'd chosen to take the cooler route as well.

Still, Eliza couldn't miss the tightening of his Adonis-like features when he mentioned that night. She refused to be affected by it. "Don't worry, I got the full story when it aired- what was the title? *Success and Scandal?* Catchy."

Cousteau let his jaw clench doing whatever it took to keep his own considerable anger from ruining his opportunity. "Everything I discovered didn't make it into the story Elly."

"Oh? Will there be a part two?" She laughed wildly.

Losing one of the restraints on his temper, he bounded toward her. "This isn't funny, dammit."

Eliza sobered in an instant. "You're so right. I should know since I tried to find the humor in it all when I realized you'd only been seeing me to verify your research."

"Is that what your mother told you, El?" He snapped, allowing his anger the advantage then.

Her palm itched with the need to slap him. Admirably, she decided calm would fit the situation much better. "*That* was the one thing she didn't have to tell me Cousteau." She smirked, her striking blues raking his form with a mix of hurt and hate. "You really didn't have to go to the trouble of sleeping with me to get the goods on my family. I'd have probably told you anything you wanted without the role in the hay." She shrugged. "Guess you'll never know."

Cousteau appeared to lose several inches off his height when her words weakened his legs and he slumped back. "You think that's why...I love you....I never stopped." He breathed.

"Damn you," she breathed back. "Say whatever the hell it is you came to say and get out."

After a few moments of still and quiet, Cousteau's bright gaze faltered and he cleared his throat. "You said my sleeping with you to research the story was the one thing your mother *didn't* have to tell you. Exactly what *did* she tell you?"

"Why?"

"I never had the chance to tell you everything I found out." He gave a flip shrug and pushed a hand into his pocket. "Just wondered if Jessica had seen fit to do so."

Bewildered, Eliza threw up her hands. "Dammit Cousteau why in the world would my mother-"

"Because she knew, Elly. She knew it all."

"Knew all what?"

Cousteau swallowed and walked away to put space between them. He knew he'd have to get it out in one quick statement then go back and add the details later. He only prayed she wouldn't throw him out on his ass before he could finish.

***

Kamari felt so anxious when she got to Eliza's that she didn't think to use the doorbell but instead rapped on the front door in a frantic manner. Vaguely, she considered the time and prayed she wasn't disturbing her friend (or her friend's unexpected guest) at such an early hour.

Still, she had to talk. Not that she wanted to tell tales out of bed regarding Huron Base's sexual skills which were nothing short of extraordinary. But now that she knew that, there left the small matter of where things stood between them. She hadn't been using her job or his past as only excuses to keep their relationship from becoming intimate. His past and her job were both very real factors that could present very real obstacles if they tried to make more of their involvement than it already was. She only needed someone to hear her ramble about the matter. Eliza was the only person-save her mother- who knew all her darkest secrets. Kam could think of no one better to act as her sounding board.

When the front door opened, Kam was all prepared to apologize to Eliza for waking her so early. The last person she expected to see on the other side of the door was Jessica Breck.

"Mrs. Breck," Kam's voice was hushed, her eyes unable to mask her surprise, "I um…I'm sorry, I didn't expect to see you here." There was a quick jerk in her chest. "Is El alright?"

Jessica moved back from the door. "She's just fine, Kamari," she waved to urge Kam inside.

"I'm sorry for interrupting." Kam's voice was still slow, still tinged with surprise.

"No worries, love. I just got here myself."

Kamari's next thoughts were that things had gone terribly wrong with Cousteau Morgan. Before she could serve up the question, Kam saw Eliza on the stairway leading down into the living room.

"Kam, glad you're here. Both of you come on in."

Kam hitched a thumb across her shoulder. "I didn't mean to interrupt. I can always come back-"

Eliza was raising a hand while making her way to one of the deep chairs in the room. "I need you to stay. I need you to stay and hear this." The last words seemed to have taken on a hushed tone.

"Honey did anything happen when Cousteau brought you home?" Kam was beginning to feel sick with guilt over not handling the task herself.

"Cousteau? Cousteau Morgan?" Jessica blurted.

Eliza laughed. "You know of another one, Mom? Sit before you fall, Mom."

Kam took a closer look at Jessica Breck then. The woman wore an expression that could best be described as horrified. Slowly, Kam smoothed hands over the sides of her jeans and took a seat on the corner of the same sofa Jessica now occupied.

"Eliza what's going on?" Kam noted her friend was still dressed in the black yoga pants and T-shirt from the previous day. "Does this have something to do with Cousteau?"

"Oh it has quite a bit to do with him."

Jessica was looking around the room and across her shoulder. "Where is he?" She asked.

Again, Eliza laughed. "Don't worry, Mom. He's not here. He only came to tell me what you wouldn't give him the chance to two years ago."

"God," Jessica moaned and covered her mouth.

"Alright El, what the hell is all this?" Kam hoped the steel in her voice would produce some results.

"'Fine Lines'. Ring a bell?"

"No." Kam said.

Eliza however was posing the question to her mother. "'Fine Lines', Mom?"

Jessica only shook her head unable to verbally respond.

"It rang a bell with Simon though, didn't it?" Eliza referred to her deceased cousin and leaned back in the chair while the question loomed. "He heard about it on one of his Vegas trips, didn't he? I guess it really is a small world, huh Mom? Or maybe your old employers just make a habit of keeping tabs on their former…stars."

"Eliza please," Jessica finally managed speech and slanted a quick look toward Kam.

Eliza leaned forward again quickly. "What? Surely you don't mind Kamari knowing? Hell, she knows more about our family scandals than I'm sure she can stand, doesn't she Ma?"

"Eliza-"

"Besides, Daddy knew. I can't think you'd mind now who else does."

Curiosity weighing out over her uncertainty, Kam inched a bit closer to the edge of the sofa. "Eliza what is this? What's this about?"

"'Fine Lines' is a business Kam. A studio specializing in…fine films, right Mom? Of course how *fine* they are sort of depends on one's individual tastes." She rolled her eyes away from Jessica. "It's a porn studio, Kam. Jessica Breck-Jessica Jackson before she married my father, was one of their most popular performers."

Jessica slammed down her fists. "Eliza that's enough!"

"Oh gosh, sorry Mom. I guess you'd prefer to go by your stage name. What was it? Juicy Jessica, that's right."

"Eliza don't," Kamari spoke up for Jessica then.

Eliza showed no sympathy for her mother who sat crying like a child on the sofa. "Simon found out and threatened to tell Dad unless you continued funding his habit, right? My cousin didn't realize that my Mom isn't about giving away money even if it's to hide some old filth from her past. You killed him, didn't you?" Her voice went eerily quiet. "I actually accused Daddy. He was acting so strange when I went to confront him about that money for Simon's therapist. I figured he was nervous over being caught but that wasn't it. He'd already figured out that *you'd* done it." Eliza leaned closer to Jessica. "Simon had the last laugh though, didn't he? Sent Daddy a copy of one of your…releases-guess he knew you pretty well after all."

"Eliza how in hell do you know all this?"

Eliza rolled her eyes toward Kam. "Cousteau told me what he found." She cut her stare back to Jessica. "That's why you insisted on me getting him out of my life when you discovered he was a reporter. Made me a pariah in the family. I felt like the slut who'd sold family secrets for a good lay when you were the biggest slut of all. But even after he told me what he knew...I still didn't believe it. Not until I got a visit from Uncle Samuel later after Cousteau left." She gave a sad smile when her mother's eyes snapped to her face. "Guess you never realized how much he really hated you." She raked all ten fingers through her hair and scrubbed at the blonde mass until her strength seemed to give out.

"He accepted you because he loved dad- especially for the way dad looked out for Simon. The other day when he found you rifling around in Dad's desk, he already knew what you were looking for." Eliza reached down next to her chair then and passed Kam a large manila envelope. "One of the detectives on the scene was a friend of my Dad's." She explained when Kam fixed her with a blank look.

"When he realized what that was, he passed it on to my uncle. Sam said the man told him he felt like the Breck shit storm was blowing hard enough without adding *that* to the mix."

Kamari retrieved a videotape from inside. The cover featured a younger Jessica Breck. 'Juicy Jessica' was shown in an array of lurid shots with an array of men.

"The writing on the envelope is Simon's." Eliza confirmed. "I remember Daddy saying that he wouldn't let any of this touch me." Her mouth trembled on the wake of a sob. "I thought he meant killing Simon, but after he got that tape he must've known you'd done it. Once I came and accused him...maybe I put the idea in his head..." Eliza shook the possibility from her mind. "Guess he'd forgotten about the tape in the drawer beneath his sofa. Maybe he even hoped somehow it'd come around and stab you in the back."

The softness and tears in Eliza's stare held the question she soon posed to her mother. "Did you think we'd hate you, Mom? Dad and me? Did you think we'd disown you because you had this in your past?"

"Oh Eliza please stop being so naïve!" Jessica snapped then, her eyes suddenly ablaze with anger instead of terror. "Your father's *family* would've spit on me as soon as look at me. I was blonde, with big boobs, no education and they could've choked on the fact that Gary chose me instead of all those frigid snobs they had picked out for him. They snubbed me before they even met me I think, looking down their noses at me because I couldn't trace my family coming over on the fucking Mayflower." She laughed a little and settled back on the sofa.

"Oh they never openly snubbed me before Gary but behind his back...oh behind his back I was just one of a stream of dumb bitches who'd managed to get pregnant and wrangle a marriage proposal." She cast a wicked glance at the envelope resting between her and Kamari. "When Cousteau Morgan came round with his research project, part of me was glad because I thought finally, *finally* these bastards would have their sordid pasts come out in the wash."

She leaned forward then, pressing a fist to her forehead as the worry returned to her eyes. "Then he came to me with what he found and expected me to believe him when he said he had no intention of revealing it in the story."

"And that's why you made me feel like dirt for being with him-made me push him out?" Eliza appeared as drained as the sound of her voice.

"We didn't know anything about him, Eliza! How could you trust him?!"

El's voice was barely above whisper level. "I've known you all my life, Mom and right now I trust you about as far as I can throw you." She looked down at her hands dangling between her thighs. "I trusted you then over everything including Cousteau's love for me and *that* was the realest thing in my life. All you cared about was saving *your* way of life."

"You're my daughter Eliza. I do love you."

"And what about Daddy? He killed himself to protect you and what were you doing after he died? Looking for that tape- trying to protect *yourself* again!"

Jessica appeared defeated once more. "You don't understand. I was trying to protect all of us."

"I want you to get out."

"Eliza-"

"Unless you're about to walk out of here and own up to what you did, I don't want to see you again."

"I loved you and Garrick," Jessica swore, her hands trembling as she worked to hold them clenched in her lap. "You two were the most important things in my life and I would've done anything-anything to protect you." She swallowed, took her purse from the coffee table and stood. "I hope you understand that one day, Baby." She turned with a resigned smile in place. "Take care of her Kamari."

Eliza waited for the door to close behind her mother and then let her tears rush in a flood.

"Honey let me help you upstairs to bed." Kam suggested when she felt the crying spell had run its course.

Eliza shook her head. "I've rested enough." She stood. "I need to get started on my father's funeral, then I've got a job to get back to."

"And what about Cousteau?"

Eliza seemed to shudder. "I'm too afraid to let myself put hope in that."

"Do you expect him to just walk away?" Kam smiled at the light she saw emerging on her friend's face.

Eliza's smile broke through-albeit wavering. "God, I hope not." She confessed and joined Kam on the sofa.

"And what about Jessica? What she did to Simon?"

"My uncle said he was going to the cops today-guess it's only a matter of time before they go knocking on her door."

"She could be on her way out of the country." Kam warned, brushing her fingers across the envelope. "She's got means, there's no need for her to even dot her own doorstep again."

Eliza shrugged, a pitiful smile curving her mouth. "What kind of daughter would I be if I hadn't given my own mother a head start?"

Kamari expelled a short laugh and flopped back on the comfy navy and mauve sofa. "I have to tell you El, I think there's more to her story. I've known her a long time and she doesn't strike me as a woman without conscience. In spite of everything, I know she loved you and your dad. I don't think she was faking that."

"Can we stop talking about this now?" Eliza was forcing herself not to cry again.

Kam muttered an apology and gave her best friend a tight squeeze. "Why don't I fix us a couple of hot teas and something to eat? Besides, I've got my own drama to share." She was about to stand when El held her tight.

"Honey what-"

"There's more. I asked about this 'Fine Lines'." Her gaze wavered past Kam's shoulder only a second. "While Cousteau gave me the run down, he told me it was a subsidiary of Base Holdings- as in Huron Base."

Kamari seemed to wilt. Then, she started to chuckle as the full scope of the news penetrated her mind.

Book III
Layers of Hate

LLL

The Breck family, along with their friends, employees and other associates anticipated the frenzied atmosphere that would surround Garrick Breck's funeral. They opted for a graveside ceremony, not about to feed the media's hunger with a parade of cars from the church to the cemetery.

Everyone there connected with the family retained stoic, emotionless expressions. There were no murmurs of grief, only the soft uplifting words from Garrick's pastor.

Kamari had arrived late and was unable to get a spot near Eliza who sat as emotionless as anyone. Kam's heart ached for her friend knowing she not only mourned the loss of her father but of her mother as well.

In a move that surprised everyone, Jessica Breck turned herself in to the cops, made a statement and refused bail even though a slew of top attorneys came to her rescue once word circulated about her actions. Jessica wouldn't let herself be helped and opted to remain in police custody until a trial date was set.

The attorneys were hard at work on her defense, deciding to make lemonade out of lemons. They were going to use the woman's choice to be a guest of the county as grounds for an insanity defense.

Even amidst her family, Eliza looked so alone and Kamari wondered how much trauma she could sustain before she simply gave up-gave out. She decided to turn her attention on the pastor's words but not before she caught a glimpse of Huron seated a few rows behind the Breck entourage.

Kamari blinked away quickly then. They hadn't seen one another since they...Huron wouldn't spend the night and Kam was glad. She didn't have a chance to talk with El about everything she was feeling. Still, the last few days had given her a chance to accept the fact that she and Huron had simply acted on attraction- nothing more.

Deciding to keep things simple eased Kam's mind...a bit. She'd feel a lot more at ease once she got Huron's take on the situation. Focusing on the *situation* at hand, she tuned in on the rest of the service.

Eliza was extending her arms to Kam- accepting the hug from her best friend.

"Are you ready to get out of here?" Kam was asking when they separated.

"Um..." Eliza produced a weak yet happy smile. "I'm actually on my way out of town."

Folding her arms across her chest, Kam tilted her head in question. Then she followed the line of El's gaze and saw Cousteau making his way through the crowd.

"Oh."

"Kam please don't give me a hard time about this, alright?" Eliza bit her lip while admiring Cousteau's stride. "I'm on edge enough about just *running off* with him after everything..."

"Hey?" Kamari tugged the sleeve of El's shirtwaist blazer. "I want you to go and forget *everything*, you hear? Focus on yourself and Cousteau like you've been wanting to for over two years now."

Eliza shook her hair across her shoulders and cast tear-moistened eyes toward the sky. "Am I that transparent?" She sighed.

"You don't wanna know." Kam kissed her cheek. "Go have fun. I promise all this drama will be waiting right here for you when you get back."

"That's what I'm afraid of." Eliza rolled her eyes. "Kam please call if there's anything…anything new about my mother."

"Count on it." Kam drew her friend into another hug.

"Hey Kam," Cousteau was approaching just as the two women pulled out of their embrace. "You ready to go, Elly?"

Eliza was already nodding. "Hello Huron." Her smile brightened.

Kam turned as well, barely able to nod when his dazzling greens settled on her.

"Cousteau, this is Huron Base." Eliza was beginning the introductions when she noticed Cousteau's grin.

"We know each other, sweet." Cousteau kissed El's cheek and then shook hands with Huron as they hugged.

"Good to have you back." Huron's greeting was soft.

The greeting mirrored the look in Cousteau's turquoise stare when he winked. "Good to be back."

Something in their expressions intrigued Kam so much that her eyes narrowed in suspicion.

"Bye Kam," Eliza was hugging her friend again. "I'll call," she promised kissing Kam's cheek before she and Cousteau bustled off.

"May I have a minute? Or are you still ignoring me?" Huron was asking once they stood off alone.

Kamari would have argued but at his daring look she chose to let the subject drop.

"Did you drive?"

Kam tilted her head in the direction of her truck parked in line with the rest of the vehicles lining the circumference of the cemetery drive. With a huff she dug into her skirt pocket when he extended his hand for the keys.

"Graham?" Huron was greeting his driver by cell while guiding Kam through the maze of funeral attendees. "I'm taking Ms. Grade home in her car. I'll call you later."

Kamari silently commended herself on remaining quiet. She planned to remain so, at least until they approached her ride.

There she opened her mouth to talk and was promptly set back against her truck and kissed most thoroughly. Seconds later, or was it minutes? Kam wondered when Huron raised his head.

"Later, alright?" he requested simply and waited for her nod before escorting her into the truck.

***

"I'm really not in the mood to eat." Kam was saying a half hour later when Huron pulled to a stop before the V Café.

He made no move to let on that he'd heard her. Once the engine was shut, he left the car and headed round to open her door.

"Now why have you been ignoring me?" Huron asked once they'd secured a back table in the busy café.

Kamari took a moment to size him up in the tailored black double breasted coat which further emphasized the striking breadth of his shoulders. "We don't exactly run in the same circles, you know?"

Huron toyed with a rolled napkin. "But that flies out the window once love's been made, right?"

Momentarily, Kam succumbed to the shiver his words sent surging. "Is that what we did?"

Feeling the slight but steady stroking of his temper, Huron managed to hold his next words until the waiter took their drink orders.

"I hope you're not going to sit there and tell me that was sex only?"

"Do you know how long we've known each other?" She countered, glancing warily at his fingers now clenching the napkin. "How could anything more emotional come into it that soon?" She stiffened when he suddenly moved in to cup her chin in his hand.

"I know what 'just sex' feels like Kamari. That wasn't it."

"What are you saying?"

"Bourbon straight and Vodka tonic." The waiter announced, having returned with their drinks.

God was she really ready to hear him say he loved her?
Kam watched Huron calmly sip from his glass. Was *he* really
ready to admit it?

"Was it my imagination or were you really not all that
surprised to see Cousteau earlier?" She swiftly changed the course
of the conversation.

Huron shrugged, the sensual curve of his mouth turning
down just slightly. "Word of everything goin' on with the Brecks
was bound to reach him."

"But that's not what brought him back, is it?" She pushed
her glass aside and set her elbows in its place. "Admit it, you
called him here because I was spending just a little too much time
with Eliza. It kept interfering with our...making love, right?" She
indulged in a bit of her drink satisfied when she saw his jaw
tighten.

"Right," He offered a smile when her gaze flickered to his.
"How about a little honesty on your part now," He paused to throw
a wave toward the restaurant's proprietor Vanessa Hale when she
caught his eye near the front of the café. His attention returned to
Kam in a second. "Are you trying to tell me you don't want to go
to bed with me again?"

Kamari swallowed an easy lie and delivered the hard truth.
"No Huron. No, I'm not telling you that."

Satisfied, Huron leaned back to enjoy his drink. Kamari did
the same. The waiter returned for their orders and Huron had to
smile when he heard her ask for the quiche. There was a quick
flash of their first meeting then. The ride they shared in his car and
the quiche he fed her.

Kamari smiled and thanked the waiter before he left with
two quiche orders. "So tell me, would you be upset if I asked to
keep things about sex- *making love* only?" She enjoyed her drink
while the question hung above.

Huron had to set his drink aside lest he crush the glass.
"Damn right I'd be upset. Beyond it," His fist slamming the table
made everything jump. "What the hell do you think I take you
for?"

She blinked, realizing just how upset he was. "Huron-"

"Shut up. So you find it appealing to be fuck buddies instead of anything more?"

"Listen I'm sorry." She let the apology loom until he assumed a more relaxed position. "I could have put that better but I know anything *more* might be out of the question if I dig deeper into something I've just discovered."

Huron went still then- deadly so.

"Did you know about Jessica Breck's past? The artistic part?" She forced herself to ask.

"What the hell are you talking about?" A frown creased his brow after several moments.

Her response had to wait, for the waiter had returned with their food.

"Thanks so much for turning me onto this," Kam had the nerve to take time sampling the quiche while Huron fumed. She eventually took note of his fingers drumming on the table top. The incredible quiche would have to wait.

"Eliza turned away from Cousteau before he could tell her all he'd discovered two years ago. The information never made it into the story and it's why Jessica was so hell bent on getting him out of town." Kam paused to fork a bit of quiche into her mouth. "She didn't mind Breck family secrets being revealed, but not her own. Jessica Breck made porn films before she married Garrick."

Huron began to massage his jaw. His gaze remained focused.

"She hid it successfully before she managed to get out." Kam spoke around another forkful of quiche. "She thought it was far behind her after so many years until her tense relationship with Simon interfered. In Vegas he found out what she'd been, threatened to blackmail her with it. It's why she killed him."

Huron sat quietly, assessing what he'd been told. Then, he smiled- a dangerous, humorless smile that silenced Kam when she saw it. Shrugging, he reached for his nearly empty glass.

"You'll have to excuse me for having a one-track mind," he drained the glass, "but what the hell does this have to do with our relationship being sex only?"

"The studio she worked for was called 'Fine Lines'. Not much has changed about them over the years except that they're now a part of Base Holdings."

Acknowledgement filtered his molten green stare. "I see...and you just can't be with a man connected to such things."

"Dammit Huron, that's not it!" Kam rolled her eyes at his thick-headedness. "Hell, I've probably got more than a few 'Fine Lines' releases in my private movie collection."

Silence swelled and Kamari indulged in a mental pat on her back for succeeding in unsettling him. She'd never seen him more surprised.

"This is about looking into something Jessica said while Eliza was sharing all this." Kam pretended not to notice his reaction to her *private* movie stash. Her expression sobered. "She kept saying that she'd done all this to protect them. She said it at least twice and she was terrified when she said it."

Huron thanked the waiter who'd arrived with a fresh drink. "What are you thinking?"

"You can blame my trouble shooter's suspicion on it but there's more to all this. For Jessica Breck to simply resign herself to a cell in county makes no sense."

"Have you considered maybe the woman's tired of living the lie?" Huron chose to play devil's advocate. "She killed Simon and knows she has to answer for it. Maybe this is her way of trying to do that."

"She's scared of that company, Huron."

His laughter drew quite a bit of feminine interest. "It's porn Kam. She was one of its stars. Anyone with a high society lifestyle would be afraid of that coming out."

"I need to know."

Huron nodded. "And this is where I take my exit."

Kam fidgeted with the lacy shirt cuff peeking out of her jacket sleeve. "I have a bad feeling about this."

"And a bad feeling about me?"

"No." She spoke without hesitating. "I would have never slept with you if that was the case. But I have to know and that could cause friction between us, you have to know that."

"And yet you want to keep sleeping with me?"

She gave a cocky tilt of her head. "Sex is basic, primal. I'm sure neither of us would be thinking of outside drama while enjoying one another in bed."

"And you really believe that?" His dangerous smile had returned. "You wouldn't be thinking of what you feel for me- what goes beyond sex when you've got me inside you."

"Stop," she practically moaned and focused on the quiche as if that would clear the scandalous throb at her core.

"I won't stop because I don't believe you."

"Why? Because I'm a woman and would never sleep with a man to satisfy lust?"

Huron only waved off her question. He wouldn't tell her their night together told him precisely that. He couldn't dwell on that night for long anyway. Reminiscing over being inside her would only have his cock throbbing in a few more seconds. He'd bowed out of the argument because regardless of all *her* arguments; all her reasoning, Kamari was his-every caramel toned curvy inch of her.

***

Lunch continued silently much to Kam's delight. The quiche; though lukewarm by the time she and Huron finished talking, was still to die for. They chatted briefly with Vanessa Hale- co-owner of the café and then settled into her truck for the drive to her condo.

"Thanks," Kam pocketed her keys when Huron handed them over. "Can I uh...can I get you anything while you wait?"

Smirking over her subtle request that he call for his car, Huron followed her into the kitchen.

"Can I get you a drink?" Kamari rushed around the kitchen taking glasses from the cabinet and giving them a quick rinse in the sink. She turned when he didn't answer and found them right there in front of her. Her body hummed in approval when he pulled her into his solid frame.

Kam didn't know what she was opening her mouth to say just there. Whatever it was, she wasn't given the opportunity.

The kiss was delving, seeking and the drive of his tongue against hers was yet another reminder of how he felt inside her-stiff, stimulating and seductive. She moaned- loud and often while insinuating herself as close as possible and taking an eager participation in the sultry act.

Eventually Huron had taken Kam by the arms and unexpectedly set her away.

"Would it matter to you to know that I've got no working ties to that studio? It was one of my first acquisitions and all I really know is the product they provide and how much money I make from it."

"Huron, you don't-"

"But I do," He shook his head while his stunning greens roamed the length of her. "I won't lose...whatever this is because of my business or my past Kamari." A muscle flexed wickedly along his jaw. "Before it's all said and done, you'll know me as well as I know you."

Kamari blinked. The statement hit home like a wrecking ball in her chest. She'd spent so much time stressing over *his* past, she hadn't stopped to think about hers.

Huron dipped his head. "Did I say something? What?" He wouldn't let up even when she shook her head. "What did I say Kam?"

"Huron..."

He straightened, releasing her arms and forcing himself not to press the issue further.

"You're not the only one with a past, Mr. Base." Her smile was a little sad. "Everyone has secret or two they'd prefer never to come to light, right?"

Huron took a step back and recalled their conversation about Jessica Breck. "You've got me curious. I dig when I'm curious too." He warned her.

"Then we have that in common."

Huron moved close again to tower. "That a challenge?"

"No. I dislike having my background poked into as much as you do."

"Yet you do it anyway."

"For my job. What would be *your* reason?"

He crowded her then so much that she could scarcely take a breath. "My reasons are way better."

"Huron-"

"Basic and primal, remember?"

Kam bit her lip. Having her supposed views on sex thrown back at her caused her to stifle any comment.

The innocent gesture tore away the final restraint on Huron's self control.

Kamari would have slipped right to her kitchen floor had she not been in his arms. He kissed her out of her chic black suit right there and carried her naked toward her bedroom. He only made it as far as the living room however, where he took her on the sofa, having only unzipped his pants.

"No protection...I'm sorry Kam," he said while they lay sated and panting on the sofa. Raising up, he braced his weight on one elbow and looked down into her face. "I've never done that...I'd never hurt you regardless of what my past tells you."

She was momentarily silenced by the force in his words, but eventually managed a nod. "I'm tested every year in spite of the fact that my sex life is a laugh."

"Thanks Kam," he intentionally misunderstood and then smiled when she began to laugh. "I test every year too even though the same goes for the state of my sex life. What?" He inquired of the look she flashed him.

"You'll never get me to believe *your* sex life's a laugh."

He remained serious. "Once you've experienced sex with emotion, yeah Kami all the rest is a laugh."

Kamari's breath was caught effectively in her throat then. She snuggled into their kiss hardly registering Huron standing and carrying her to her bedroom.

***

"What are you talking about?" Eliza almost laughed when Cousteau's voice filled the room. He'd asked her what was wrong. Funny, since he was presently lying with his head on her bare abdomen and unable to see her face.

"Why would you think something's wrong?" She nudged his head with her thigh.

"I can feel your stomach tighten." He trailed a finger across a tiny mole on the otherwise alabaster tone of her thigh. "You only do that when you're tense."

Eliza closed her eyes. "I could be aroused, you know?" She purred though silently she thought how nice it was to have someone who knew you so well. She smiled when she felt him chuckling.

"I'm not doing anything to arouse you just now."

"You're lying on my tummy, Cou."

He raised his head. "Is that all it takes? After all this time?"

Eliza tugged a hand through the thickness of his glossy brown hair. Her expression was answer enough.

Raising above her, Cousteau enticed her into a sultry kiss.

"Now tell me what's up?" He insisted when they came up for air.

Tired of denying it, Eliza inched up in the king bed facing the picture windows with their view of the Pacific. "I'm worried for my mother and I hate myself for it after all she's done."

Cousteau dropped a kiss to her shoulder. "She's your mother, Elly."

"It's because of her that we lost two years." Eliza drew her knees to her chest and wrapped her arms about her legs. "She had the family treating me like an outcast when she found out about us-why you were here…all because she didn't want that…studio crap to come out."

"Hell love, can you blame her?"

"No." Eliza replied with no hint of hesitation. She shrugged and raised her brows in a saucy manner. "Actually, it's pretty cool."

Cousteau raised a brow that time.

Eliza brought her index finger within inches of his nose. "I dare you to deny it." She smiled when he shrugged. "All my life, my mom was this- this image I tried to aspire to. Perfection- always dressed just right for the occasion, saying the right things, conversing knowledgeably about any subject on the table…" She rolled her eyes and sighed. "I'm probably the only woman in the world who wanted to be just like her mother."

Cousteau toyed with a blonde lock clinging to the cuff of her ear.

Eliza's gaze clouded. "But for all that…perfection, she never seemed totally real to me. Maybe that's why- because she was so perfect."

"What are you trying to say?" Cousteau smoothed back her hair and studied her alluring profile.

"The other day, she seemed so scared…frightened, Cousteau." El turned to look at him.

"Ah Babe, people don't always take it well when their past comes back to haunt them."

"Wasn't that." Eliza's voice was whisper soft. "She said she did what she did to protect us- me and dad. The way she said it…I don't know." She tossed her hair as if trying to remove the thoughts.

"You want to go to her?"

Eliza shut her eyes against the beauty of the coastal view. They'd spent a few memorable days basking in the beauty of Cousteau's Malibu escape. Eliza craved many more of those days but knew she wouldn't fully enjoy it until she had answers.

"I have to know what she's afraid of."

***

Tenille Yancy was as speechless as every other woman in the offices of Grade Business Securities when Huron Base walked up to her desk. She could see his mouth moving- *boy what a mouth*... Vaguely she noted that he must have been talking; but with the buzzing in her ears, she couldn't hear a thing.

Thankfully, her ears unclogged and her tongue loosened in time for the man not to think she was a complete idiot.

"I'm sorry Mr. Base?"

Huron grinned. "Is Ms. Grade in?" He repeated.

Tenille's mouth turned down. "I'm sorry Mr. Base but she's left town. Left this morning. She came to the office for some things, left instructions..."

Huron fought to hide the tightening in his jaw. He could see it in Kamari's eyes the night before. She was withdrawing. When he woke alone in her bed that morning, he hadn't even been surprised. Still, the fact that she'd high-tailed it out of town had him more than concerned. Tuning back into Tenille, he decided using a larger amount of his considerable charm was definitely warranted then.

"Did she by any chance leave word on when she'd be back? More preferably, did she leave word on where she was going? I'd really be very grateful to know, Tenille." His green eyes crinkled slightly at the corners when he smiled.

Tenille didn't need to be any more charmed than she already was. Fidgeting with the buttons on her tailored red shirt, she recalled Kam from that morning. The woman had appeared stressed out of her mind. With a husband across the world in war, Tenille knew better than anyone how much worse stress could be when you were alone. Still, she did own her boss some discretion. "She said something about dropping in on her parents."

The clue was more than enough. Huron's grin broadened and he leaned close to kiss Tenille's cheek.

The office filled with a collective sigh.

***

Aspen, Colorado~

Raven Grade topped off her daughter's coffee and then set the carafe back to its warmer. The petite woman's ratty yet comfy brown house shoes slapped merrily at the glistening hardwood floor when she moved.

Kamari took several seconds to simply enjoy the aroma of the blend. Clearly indigenous to Aspen for she'd never been able to locate the brew any place else.

"You know I'd love having you visit just once when you're not running from a case." Raven sighed when she shuffled over to rejoin Kam at the round table.

Kam raised her brows and took a sip of her coffee. "You'll be pleased to know that I'm not running from a case." Her smugness waned. "It's a relationship."

Raven's light eyes widened. "Must I spike the coffee to get you to tell me more?"

Kamari had to laugh in spite of her edginess. "I need to talk about this one Mama." She confessed.

Instantly serious, Raven squeezed Kam's wrist. "Tell me." She urged, listening actively while her daughter spoke of Huron Base and how he'd completely shattered all her preconceived notions of him.

"But honey…" Raven's round face was a picture of confusion. "Why would you run away from what sounds like the beginning of love?"

"Mama please! Love? I haven't even known him that long."

Raven tugged her mug close and smirked. "I didn't know your father that long either, remember?"

Kam remembered very well since Casper Grade had come into their lives at a time when both she and her mother were on the verge of shutting out a world that had damaged them both. Casper wasn't Kamari's biological father but of course that was less than insignificant. He was the only father she knew- the only father she wanted to know.

"The way Dad came to us wasn't the norm, Mama. It can't compare and it's not like that with me and Huron."

"Isn't it?" Raven was staring down into her half filled mug. The tendrils of her curly bob curtained a portion of her profile. "Does your reluctance have anything to do with-"

"No." Kam raised her hand on the stern denial and stood from the table.

"Honey when will you deal with this?"

"I have dealt with it." Kam's voice was thick with emotion yet her stare was distant as she studied the never ending blanket of white that covered her parent's property. "God blessed me to be well adjusted. Not misguided, seeking out abusive relationships because I..." She hissed a curse and bowed her head.

Raven rushed from the table and moved to pull her daughter back into a tight hug. "I think you're fooling yourself, Baby. I believe you only put a lid on this. It's a tight lid but lids were made to be removed. Maybe this connection with Huron Base is more intense than you think. Intense enough to make you share what's beneath the lid?"

Kam was shaking her head against her mother's neck. "I don't want him to know that. I don't want anyone to know-especially him."

"Baby..." Raven pressed a kiss to Kam's ear. "Honey I'll bet he's got a few things in his past he may not want you to know either."

Kam laughed almost hysterically then. "Mama that's a bet you'd definitely win but trust me, Huron's secrets are nothing like mine."

"Are you afraid he'd turn away from you if he knew?" Raven rested her chin on Kam's shoulder.

"Don't men often turn away once a woman's shared something like that about herself?"

"How would you know when you haven't given him a chance?"

"Hmph, I'm brave but just not brave enough to go through that."

"Not even for the man who could be the one?"

Kam thought for a moment and then shook off the possibility. "None of this matters anyway when there're tons more reasons why there'd be friction between us."

Raven sighed then and stepped away. "How does Huron feel about all these roadblocks you're throwing up?" She folded her arms across her chest and leaned against the counter.

"I'm not-" Kam turned ready to argue her point. She realized she couldn't. "He doesn't like them but he knows they're valid."

Raven gave an exaggerated shrug. "Well you know him better than I do. Do *you* believe he'll let it go at that?"

Kamari went to the table and grabbed her mug. "Does that offer to spike the coffee still stand?"

What the hell are you doing here, Base? Huron was asking himself as he drove the rented sport utility beyond the huge stone markers which announced he was entering Boulder Crest and that he was welcomed.

The division was a continuation of the snowy wonderland he'd been travelling through since settling into the SUV at the jetport.

Instead of a never-ending trail of trees and brush, the landscape was dotted with spacious homes on either side of a wide road which dead ended at the base of a breathtaking mountain range.

Was this more gutsy and smart or pompous and assumptive? He wondered. He didn't want to crowd her; but as she'd seen fit to leave the state, she left him with little choice. Sure this could have just been a quick stop on the way to investigate 'Fine Lines' but he knew better. She was running and he had to wonder whether it was from his past or her own.

Twisting his lips into a decisive smirk, Huron pressed lightly on the accelerator and continued his journey. He followed the GPS until it led him to one of the last snowy dwellings on the quiet street. His agitation grew when he spotted a white man shoveling snow from the curving brick driveway.

Obviously he'd taken a wrong turn somewhere and cursed the inaccurate piece of navigating machinery. Grumbling a curse, he tugged on his toboggan and left the truck idling. He hoped the man was a neighbor who might point him in the right direction.

The older gentleman turned at the sound of snow crunching beneath show soles. A welcoming smile spread across an attractive weather beaten face.

"Good morning." He stepped close to greet Huron with a handshake.

"I'm sorry for interrupting, but I think I'm lost." Huron admitted with an easy grin. "I pray I'm at least in the right neighborhood."

The man chuckled and took note of the surroundings. "All the houses look the same once the first big snow sets in. We should be able to make out the paint on the shudders in another seven months or so."

"It's incredible." Huron took a moment to more closely observe and then turned with uncertainty shadowing his face. "Do you have any neighbors with the last name Grade?"

The man laughed. "Sure do. Know 'em pretty well."

Huron nodded and looked around again. "Could you point me in the direction of their home? I'm hoping to speak with their daughter."

The man's gaze narrowed and lost just a bit of its warmth. "Kamari?" He queried, watching Huron nod. "I'll warn you, the father's pretty overprotective- obsessively so." He folded his hands atop the peak of the shovel's handle. "I hope your conversation with Kamari will be a nice one."

"Oh sir, it's nothing like that." Huron realized how he must have come across and silently chastised himself. "I'm only concerned- *very* concerned. She left so fast…I only want to know it wasn't because of anything I said- though I have a feeling it was."

The man nodded slow and then eventually stepped forward to clap a hand down firm on Huron's shoulder. "I guess that'll get you through the front door." Extending his hand for another shake, he introduced himself as Casper Grade.

Kam and her mother were laughing hysterically. At that point neither could remember what had sparked the giggle fest. Raven fulfilled Kamari's request for spiked coffee and went on to spike her own. Kamari was faced down on the table while tears streamed her eyes.

Casper arrived in the high curved doorway of the kitchen. Huron wasn't far behind. Casper smiled watching his wife and daughter at the table with a bottle of rum between them.

Raven was shaking hair from her eyes when she caught sight of her husband.

"I don't think this drunken display will make a good impression on Kam's young man."

Silence settled quickly. Kam pulled her head off the table and found herself staring into Huron's jade gaze. She swallowed as her buzz oozed away.

"Oh my," Raven recovered and rushed from the table.

"Raven Grade, Huron Base." Casper introduced.

Kam massaged her forehead, peeking through her fingers to observe Huron with her parents. She could read his expressions easily enough by then to know that he was taking in her mother's youthful features. People often mistook them for sisters, easy since there were only fourteen years separating them. Huron's responses to Raven's offers for food and drink were subdued as he studied she and then Kamari.

"Well you just help yourself to anything, okay?"

Huron's eyes slanted toward Kam. "Thank you, Mrs. Grade." He didn't bother to mask what was going through his mind then.

"*Mrs. Grade,* listen to you!" Raven brushed Huron's forearm and chuckled. "It's Raven, *please.*"

Huron smiled and dipped his head. "I'll remember that."

"You wanna bring the bottle?" Casper was teasing his wife as they left the kitchen.

"Damn that Tenille." Kam grumbled once they were alone.

"She didn't tell me exactly where you were. Only gave me a hint." Huron explained, taking the seat in the chair Raven had just vacated.

"What are you doing here?"

"Only what Ms. Raven told me." He moved close, grabbed Kam's chair by a leg and pulled it close.

Kam's hands splayed across his thighs, chest and shoulders. She concluded the wanton display by raking her fingers through his hair and actually inched closer with intentions of positioning herself on his lap.

Huron brought the kiss to an end however. Though he craved her kisses, he was far more interested in having his questions answered. He pulled her hands from his hair and squeezed while giving her a tiny jerk to rouse her from her daze.

"What are *you* doing here?"

She shrugged, focusing on the BOSS logo emblazoned across the white sweatshirt he sported. "Visiting my parents."

Huron clenched his jaw, deciding not to ask the slew of questions he knew she was expecting him to hurtle toward her. "Why did you run from me?"

Kamari couldn't response, not even to deny.

"Did I say something wrong, Kam?" He dropped his stare when she fixed him with a frown. "What I said about knowing you as well as you know me. That's why you ran, isn't it?" he tilted his head trying to recapture her gaze. "As concerned as you are about our businesses butting heads, it's not what scares you most, is it?"

Kam stood and went to look past the windows above the chrome double sink.

"After all you've found out about me, what is it about you that you think I won't understand?"

Kamari kept her back to him. "I haven't learned the half about you." She shook her head. "So don't try acting like you've laid all your cards on the table the way you expect *me* to."

Huron left the table. "At least I'm willing to acknowledge that it'll happen sooner or later."

"I'm banking on later." Kam bit her lip when she felt him standing behind her.

Huron knew she was being purposefully difficult because she was afraid. It riled him just the same. "Don't shut me out." He made her face him then.

Kamari tried to wrench away. "Where's all this coming from?" She snapped when he wouldn't allow her release. "And so soon? We haven't known each other any time at all."

"Funny. That's what I'm trying to do and what *you* keep avoiding."

"Stop. We haven't known each other long enough to be sharing our darkest secrets."

Huron let go of Kam and stepped back looking as though he were satisfied. "So it is a *dark* secret?"

Kamari grabbed a few curls and made a pretense at screaming.

Huron relished it. Leaning close again, he kissed her temple. "That'll do for now."

Kam watched in sheer wonder as he turned and left the kitchen.

Several hours later, Huron Base had effectively charmed Casper and Raven Grade. The couple had insisted on Huron taking the second guest bedroom- much to Kamari's unease. Kam of course knew running was out of the question.

Huron had experienced a deep sense of glee when he realized he'd not only blocked in her rental with his, but that the road leading to the Grade's development had been closed due to the snow until the next afternoon at least.

Raven was staring past her kitchen windows watching the two men tour the back yard.

"My goodness, that Huron is an incredible thing to look at."

Kam seated again at the kitchen table, wadded a paper towel and threw it at the back of her mother's head. "You already have an incredible thing to look at."

"Ah..." Raven's gaze narrowed devilishly. "But the good thing about your father is that I get to do more than look."

"I'm gonna be ill." Kam groaned.

Raven laughed, speed walking to the table to slap her daughter's shoulder. "Girl why are you fighting this? He seems wonderful and I can tell he's very into you."

"Mama do you even care about what's beneath all that?" Kam fell back on her standard reasoning.

"Course I do." Raven gave a one-shoulder shrug. "It's *you* who doesn't seem to be interested in finding out."

The words smarted and Kam couldn't even tell her mother than she was right.

"It's incredible, but I'll bet it can be a big inconvenience." Huron remarked on the weather while standing more than ankle deep in the show that was still falling.

Casper chuckled while nodding his agreement. "You come from a cold climate?"

"Lived in California all my life," Huron shared. "Visited the mountains a time or two when I was a kid- more now that I'm an adult."

"This is all I've ever known, til a trip out West one year changed all that." Casper was saying, his deep set gaze easy yet reminiscent. "It's where I met Raven and Kam Kam."

"They look more like sisters than mother and daughter." Huron took advantage of the opening to quell his curiosity about the women.

"Rave had Kam when she was fourteen." Casper's stare was still reminiscent but something a bit tense now lurked in his pitch gaze.

"That's gotta be tough." Huron winced thinking of his own mother then. "Did Ms. Raven know the father?"

Casper's smile was both honest and proud. "She knew me."

Huron produced a proud smile of his own and decided against further probing. He simply figured there may have been some ex-lover tensions floating about and left it at that.

There wasn't time for more talk as Raven was calling then for them to come in from the cold.

***

After a filling dinner of hearty beef stew and corn bread muffins, Casper and Raven decided to turn in early; making a none too subtle attempt at giving the younger couple time alone.

Kam thought of using the 'turning in early' excuse herself but had a sneaking suspicion that Huron would follow her up...and inside.

They shared coffee before the fire with smooth jazz softly filling the lower level. For a time, the crackling flames, music and clink of spoons in mugs were the only sounds in the room.

"I've got a criminal record, Kamari. I realize you already know that."

Kam felt a slight shiver beneath the fuzzy peach fabric of her oversized sweater. "I only found some relatively petty scuffles-I've got the feeling you'd pulled some very heavy strings to keep the more...heinous acts a secret."

Huron propped chin to fist and set her a sideways glance. "I'm surprised you didn't dig deeper to find out what they were."

Kam snuggled deeper into the chair and a half she occupied. "I figured I had enough to dissuade the Brecks from doing business with you."

"That means you don't want to know?" Huron sipped at the still piping hot coffee.

Kam set her mug to an end table. "I wouldn't be a very good investigator if I wasn't still curious about you." She cast a playfully skeptical look about her surroundings. "Are you prepared to share you deepest and darkest in my parent's living room?"

"I'm prepared to share everything with you."

"Why?" The whispered word was seriousness personified.

Huron shook his head as though he were confused by the 'why' as well. Then, he smoothed the back of his hand across the silk whiskers that shadowed his face. "Maybe it's just that a man'll do anything to hold onto the exquisite treat of making love to a bow-legged woman."

Kamari's laughter filled the room as she stood intent on refilling her mug. Huron caught her wrist when she walked past. He tugged her to his lap. Kam swallowed and took a moment or so before raising her eyes to his.

"I guess you can imagine the *items* on my record are long, varied and ugly." His stare faltered and he focused on inspecting her fingers. "They're not the sort of things I'd risk telling you all at once."

"So what?" Kam fought to keep her tone light and reciprocated toying with his fingers as well. "You'll trickle out the elements of your past, while I fall for you. Then when all is revealed, I'll just be too in love with you to care?"

He kept his gaze lowered. "Somethin' like that." He looked up at her then. "Actually, it's exactly like that." His free hand trapped her neck and he tugged her close.

Kamari was whimpering seconds before his mouth melded with hers. The kiss was lusty from the onset and she forgot everything except his hands on her body- journeying beneath the hem of her bulky sweater.

"I need you to leave with me." He murmured during the kiss.

Fuzzy brained from the rough power of his tongue caressing and outlining hers, Kam could barely lock onto his request.

"Leave with me, Kam."

"Why?" She managed to moan that time.

His beautifully sculpted lips were tracing her jaw then. "There's something I need to do." Those sculpted lips rested at her pulse point before lavishing the area with a wet kiss. "I want you there with me when I do it." He pulled away then. "I swear it's not illegal."

Kamari rolled her eyes while pushing at the wall that was his chest.

"If you want to satisfy your curiosity about me, this would be the perfect time to do it." He leaned in for another kiss. This one was quick and sweet, then he nudged her off his lap and left her alone in the room.

***

Eliza summoned a last measure of courage when the chrome doors opened and an armed guard led her mother into the conference room. El prayed her expression wasn't overtly horrified but she'd never seen Jessica Breck looking more unlike herself. Dressed in a standard issue jumpsuit, Jessica's eyes looked huge in her very thin face. Yet, the emotion was there when she smiled. Eliza returned the gesture without hesitation.

Jessica seemed on the verge of rushing forward to hug her daughter but cast a quick glance over her shoulder and thought better of it. Still, they clasped hands once seated across from one another at the cold table.

"Mama why won't you let the lawyers try for bail?"

"It'd be useless, honey." Jessica's smile was regretful. "With my assets, they'd consider me a flight risk."

"Maybe...but that's not the real reason, is it?" El dipped her head to follow her mother's gaze when it wavered. "What did you mean about needing to protect me and dad?"

"Why baby...his, his reputation of course."

Eliza laughed at the absurd excuse in light of where the Breck reps stood. Her heart soared when she saw a smile break through on her mother's face.

"Mama, don't you think it's time for you to tell me the truth instead of shielding me from it?"

Whatever easiness brightened Jessica's face dimmed with Eliza's words. "This is one thing I'll try to shield you from for the rest of my life."

Eliza slumped back and felt the cold seeping from the chairs metal bars and through the silk of her walnut blouse. "Do you expect me to forget this when you killed a man to keep it quiet?"

"You don't want to know these people. *I* don't want you to know these people." Jessica hissed, pointing her index finger down on the table.

"Why all the secrecy still, Mama?" Tears glossed Eliza's blur stare. "You've been Jessica Breck for decades. What could they do to you now? It's not concern for the family. Dad's...dead and...as for me- I'm a grown woman."

Jessica began to bite on her thumbnail while her daughter diminished whatever excuses she might have latched onto.

Eliza leaned over to pull her mother's hands into hers. "I love you. That won't ever change, no matter what I discover from your past."

Jessica leaned down to kiss Eliza's hands. "Thank you, baby," she breathed against them. "Honey...when I left 'Fine Lines' I-I took things."

Smirking, Eliza shrugged. "And they want them back after all this time?"

"Not material things, El- not like you think... Information." Jessica stared unseeing at one of the concrete walls that made up the room. "Things I saw, things I'm sure are still going on...I'm not the only one with secrets they'd kill to protect."

"Mama *please* let me help you." El gave Jessica's hands a vice like squeeze. "Do you really think your being in here would be a relief to them? I'm sure they're wondering what you might give up to get out."

Jessica blinked, looking then as though she hadn't considered that possibility. She closed her eyes as the reality of it all shone through. "What am I going to do then? I have to answer for Simon's death- there's no way out of that. I've lived with the rest for so long...I want to make things right."

Eliza's heart soared again at the fire and determination she'd never witnessed in her mother's eyes. Nodding, she extended both hands again and she and her mother held onto one another.

***

Two days later, Kam stood in the snow-shoveled driveway and was embraced in a double hug by her parents.

"I'm sorry to be leaving so soon." Her voice was muffled in the heavy sweaters they wore. She heard them chuckling and knew they probably understood it all better than she did.

"Daddy shouldn't you be the slightest bit suspicious of a man who follows me all the way here and who's now whisking me away again?" She asked when stepping out of the embrace.

Casper's dark gaze crinkled humorously at the corners as he watched Huron take a call near his SUV. "I got a good feeling about the kid."

Kamari shook her head toward Raven, knowing she didn't even need to ask how she felt. The woman was like a boy-crazed girl.

"I've prayed that you'd find someone strong to lean on. Not that you need that." Raven added before her daughter could argue. "But it does come in handy at times." She snuggled into her husband's lean frame and accepted the kiss he pressed to her mouth.

Kamari adored the emotion that swirled about her parents like a living thing. Her ease cooled, but didn't completely diminish when she felt Huron's hand at the small of her back.

"You ready?" His voice was soft when he leaned close to ask. At Kamari's nod, he fixed the Grade's with one of his gorgeous smiles. "Thanks so much to you both for making me feel so welcome." He was extending his hand and was stunned when the couple pulled him into a double hug.

When Casper walked back to the SUV with Huron, Raven pulled her daughter close.

"Give the boy a chance and, while you're at it, give yourself one."

"I promise Mama." Kam realized she meant it and held Raven close as they strolled toward the idling SUV.

**

Kamari was...well stunned to say the very least when she peered past the small curtained windows of the jet. The distinct area below could be mistaken for no other place in the world.

"Las Vegas?" A disbelieving smirk curved her lips. "This is why we had to make a mad dash from my parent's place?"

Huron only rested his cheek against his palm. His smile was as soft as the look of his dazzling greens. "You have a problem with Vegas?"

"Never." Kam shrugged and looked out the window again. "Had I known you wanted to gamble, I could've contacted a girlfriend out here who owns one of the newest casinos on the block." Kam set the curtains back in place over the window and reclined in her seat.

"Gambling'll be plentiful where we're going but gambling wasn't my reason for coming here."

Kamari didn't bother to inquire. Though she was boring holes through him with her curious gaze, she knew he wouldn't elaborate on his *reasons*.

"I don't have Vegas clothes," she muttered.

"Does the place require certain attire?" He laughed heartily at the strained look she threw him.

"How about I take you shopping?"

"How about you tell me why you brought me here?"

"How about somethin' better?"

Soon after, he'd tugged her to his lap and Kam decided 'somethin' better' was her favorite of the three choices.

"Can I get you to be just a little patient?" the depth of his voice had taken on an adorable softness.

Kam wouldn't thing of denying the request. Not when she was already straddling his lap, and becoming too preoccupied with the most alluring part of his anatomy. The impressive semi-hard erection nudged the single most tingling part of her and she could've melted from the friction. Discussing *anything* was becoming less and less important.

Huron; already in tune with her every reaction, smiled and smoothed the back of his hand along her jaw. His other hand smoothed up the length of her thigh and he insinuated his thumb against the part of her that he yearned for.

Blindly, Kam sought his kiss which was heat and need at once. They fondled once another scandalously until the captain announced their descent into Las Vegas and requested his passengers into their seatbelts.

***

"No..." Eliza moaned when Cousteau suggested they leave her very much utilized bed and grab some dinner.

"You want to see your mom before visiting hours are over, don't you?" Cousteau smothered her with his weight then.

Eliza snuggled in; sliding her hands up and over the sculpted plane of his chest. "Except for the two of us, I want to shut out all the rest of the world." Her blue eyes were awe-filled while surveying his muscle packed chest.

The lone dimple spliced Cousteau's cheek. "I didn't think you'd ever feel like that again."

Eliza dragged her fingers through his hair and sighed. "I didn't either and I'm so happy that things often have a way of rearranging themselves."

"That what you wish for your mom?" Cousteau asked once he'd leaned in to steal a kiss.

Eliza closed her eyes for a second and then looked up to focus on her bed room ceiling. "I wish she'd talk to me about what's upsetting her but at least she's willing to talk."

"But only to Kam?"

"Yeah..." El didn't hide the preoccupation in her eyes. "She knows how much I trust Kam. There's certainly no one in the family to go to. Except my father...Kam's the obvious choice."

"It's strange." Cousteau rolled to his back pulling El across his chest. "None of my research turned up anything more than the porn studio."

Eliza shook her head, absently scraping her nails down his chiseled abdomen. "Whatever it is, it's scaring her enough to make prison more appealing than the outside world."

***

The door to the suite swung open with Kamari in Huron's arms and kissing madly. The chopper they'd settled into once the jet set them down had carried them to the rooftop of the hotel. No sooner were they inside the elevator; which would open right in the room, was she in his arms. In spite of the privacy, Kam protested when he sought to pull her out of her clothes right there in the elevator.

Still kissing, they left the elevator and Huron made quick work relieving her of her layered clothing. Comfy when they left Colorado, Kam was roasting once they set down in Vegas. Of course she had visited the town enough to know that the sweltering heat could tone down to a less than comforting chill later that evening.

Such things however weren't her top priorities just then. With Huron's hands everywhere, Kam couldn't think. She didn't want to unless her thoughts centered on the fantastic feel of his hands on her body fast becoming free of clothing.

He deposited her nude to the center of the shamefully huge, thoroughly decadent bed. His mouth finished what his hands began. The devastating friction of his tongue thrusting and rotating inside her sex mingled with the rough sensation of his whiskers upon her inner thighs brought her to sharp orgasm.

There was no time to recover; as if she could, from the climax. Without mercy, Huron flipped her to her stomach, posed her to his satisfaction and took her from behind. Kam gripped the hand carved brass frame that was the bed's headboard while Huron cupped one of her breasts in his massive grip. His other hand curved about her thigh, his fingers manipulating the moisten folds of her center.

"Plenty of time for rest afterwards," He murmured against her ear.

"After what?" Kam summoned the strength to form the words. She was unquestionably depleted.

Huron slapped her bare bottom. "Let's take a shower."

His enthusiasm grating on her nerves, Kam only snorted and turned her face back into the pillows. Soon after the lazy display, she felt Huron's arm hook about her waist. Llike a sack of potatoes, she was carried without ceremony to the shower.

There was something a bit- okay, okay *a lot* arousing about standing behind a gorgeous man in a casino with loads of dollars before him and more on the way. Especially when you yourself looked like a piece of eye candy and few made a secret of watching you like they were eager to take a sample.

Kamari almost laughed aloud at her outlandish summations. Honestly though, she couldn't recall when she'd felt so relaxed and excited-being made love to so exquisitely not withstanding.

"You okay?" Huron murmured without looking back at her.

"Just can't believe how much fun I'm having." She confessed, her eyes sparkling while she surveyed the provocative beauty of the casino hotel. The mixture of mauves, burgundies and golds collided in a color scheme as soothing as it was seductive.

"Card," Huron instructed the dealer. "You and my opponent have something in common then." He said without raising his stare from the hand he studied.

Sharp as ever in spite of her relaxed state, Kam didn't miss the grimace when he shared the tidbit. Clearly, he'd caught sight of-and disliked- his opponent's ogling Kamari across the table.

"But not for long." Huron predicted and sounded as though he were speaking to himself.

Amazed, Kam watched him spread out the hand of cards and listened as the dealer declared him the winner.

"Having a beauty behind you at the table is always important." He said when rising from his chair.

Huron shook hands with his opponent, then passed the dealer a rectangular plate etched with $100- or perhaps it was $1000. Kam couldn't tell which.

"Is this what you needed me in Vegas for?" Her mouth curved into a playfully exasperated smile when he gave her one of the plates marked $500.

"Not exactly," Huron shoved the remaining plates to an inner pocket on his silver gray dinner jacket. Setting a hand to Kam's waist, he insinuated his fingers between one of the many straps crossing her back in an alluring array of black. He guided her through the maze of tables and bodies toward a set of double pine doors at the rear of a grand room. There, he swiped a card which granted them entrance to a quiet lengthy corridor.

Kam's amusement quelled and she grew more subdued by the area with its never ending line of closed doors. Stark and imposing, the area was the exact opposite of the exuberance of the casino.

Curiosity merged with Kam's other emotions when Huron escorted her into a spacious dim room. A woman waited there along with three other men.

Kam barely registered Huron drawing her deeper into the chic room with its suede furnishings, gleaming mahogany conference table and floor to ceiling windows that displayed Vegas at night.

"Dutch and Sandra Breslin, this is Kamari Grade." Huron made the introductions but gave the couple no chance to shake hands with Kam. Instead, he settled Kam to one of the deep charcoal colored chairs in the room.

"This is Jeffrey Kears and Steve Burns." He waved a hand toward the two men perched on the other end of the table.

Kam made no secret of being nosy and leaned forward to listen in. Huron greeted the group again and she soon ascertained that Steve Burns was his attorney. Jeffrey Kears was counsel for the Breslins. The Breslins were co-owners of 'Fine Lines Studio.'

"Thanks for bringing your lawyer, Base. Maybe he can clarify this. Sandra and I are more confused than ever." Dutch Breslin spoke up, hitching his thumbs through his trouser belt loops in a show of confrontation. "What's this sudden desire to sell your part in the studio?" He snapped his fingers toward his attorney. "The place is makin' money hand over fist." He shook the page of figures Jeffrey Kearns had passed him.

"Impressive." Huron barely scanned the sheet before tossing it to the table. "You'll be just fine without me, then."

The Breslins exchanged glances.

"So suddenly you're eager to give away millions a year?" Dutch challenged.

"My choice." Huron's voice was soft and easy as his manner. He smirked. "Just as it was my choice to come on board with you in the first place."

"This about Jessica Breck?" Dutch cast a quick glance toward Kam.

Huron's smile then held a coolness which belied a lurking but clearly existent danger.

Dutch Breslin cleared his throat, showing unease for the first time. "Could we have a moment Huron?"

When her husband walked off to a corner with Huron, Sandra Breslin walked over to Kam.

Standing, Kamari almost smiled in anticipation of hearing what the woman had to say. Sandra Breslin extended her hand for the shake they'd been denied when introduced earlier.

"Huron should never have involved you in such boring business." The woman's vivid blue stare harbored cleverness as she tilted her head. "If he's involving you though, things between the two of you must be serious." She smiled as if she'd already found the answer to that probe. She scanned Kam's petite provocatively dressed form and then regarded Huron momentarily.

"He's perhaps the most mysterious man I've ever met." Sandra's admission harbored a tone bordering on arousal. "With him being so young that only makes the mystery more provocative."

Kam only shrugged. "My guess is he'll think I'd find all this fascinating."

Sandra folded her arms over the daring scoop neckline of her gold cocktail dress. "What's your business, Ms. Grade?"

Pleased that her words provoked the intended response, Kam took a moment to study Huron as well.

"Troubleshooting investigation."

Sandra blinked, obviously stunned. "Is it as glamorous as it sounds?"

Kamari had to laugh. "I don't know about glamour, but it's never dull."

"I'm betting you're very respected in your field."

"Depends on whether you've hired me to do the investigating or whether you're the one I'm investigating."

Sandra appeared resigned. "I think *our* business would be the latter of the two." She raked perfectly manicured nails across a surgically enhanced chin. "You *are* aware of what our studio produces?"

"I'm aware."

"Then Kamari, surely you can understand our concern over Huron wanting to sell?"

Kam shrugged then. "Sandra it's not my place to understand."

"You know this isn't a simply matter of selling interest in a business." Dutch dragged a hand through his unruly crop of salt and pepper hair. "Hell, certain things have taken place that-"

"Hold on Dutch. I'm not interested in what went on here before I took part in your business."

"Simon Breck was interested." Dutch supplied, sneering when the fact was shared. "As I recall he was *very* interested and it got him killed. Now Jessica's in jail for it and thinking of doing God knows what to save her ass," he stood back a bit and smirked. "And here *you* are selling to distance yourself. Should my wife and I be dusting off our passports, Base?"

Huron had already zoned out of the conversation and was focused on Kamari.

"She's the woman I love." He confessed; almost unaware that he was even doing so. "I don't intend to lose her...ever. Surely that'll happen if we maintain ties." He turned back to Dutch. "So you can either take my very generous offer or I can very simply take the studio, sell it and you and Sandra won't even have money to head out to wherever those passports would carry you."

"Always to the point, eh?" Dutch hid both hands in his trouser pockets and smiled. "San!" He called out to his wife. "Huron's got papers for us to sign."

***

"Why didn't you tell me?"

"Talk is cheap."

Arm in arm, Huron and Kam headed down the corridor leading to their suite.

"All the money you're losing." She marveled.

"Yeah, everyone keeps reminding me of that."

"Well?"

"What?" He countered when she elbowed his side for not answering.

"Is it worth it?" Kam's vibrant browns sparkled with expectancy.

No sooner had the words left her mouth, than Huron held her pressed to a wall. He took her mouth in a sudden kiss that was arousing, deep and branding. Kam's fingers curled into the collar of his shirt and she arched closer when he made a move to break the kiss.

The lusty battle between their tongues lasted until Huron realized his hand had disappeared inside the split of her dress. Mere seconds existed between him snatching the panties from her hips and removing his hand.

"Kam," he muttered, urging her to take pity and cease torturing him with her nibbles along his jaw. When she complied he nudged her cheek with his and closed his eyes as though deep in thought.

"Is it worth it?" He repeated her question and opened his eyes to search hers. "Yes. Yes, it's most definitely worth it."

***

Dutch and Sandra Breslin remained in the casino floor conference room long after everyone else left. The couple discussed Huron and the woman he loved.

"What else do you think he'll try to get rid of?" Sandra asked her husband.

"Not sure." Once again, Dutch was raking back his hair.

Sandra glanced at the closed double doors. "You think he's trying to redeem himself for her?"

"It'd make sense."

"He's going to make a lot of people angry."

"Yes…" Dutch's expression was beyond grim, the deep tan of his square face appeared flush. "And I've got a feeling his lovely little troubleshooter's going to get caught right in the middle of it."

Hello Everyone,

I hope this three part effort of the *Layers* Series was worth the wait and that Huron Base and Kamari Grade were as strong and sexy as you expected them to be. These stories and the characters- primary and secondary- hold a different tone for me. The motivation driving them carries a powerful and mysterious current as I craft the stories. It's truly as if I'm peeling back actual layers and each new path the novel takes is really a surprise.

I hope you'll hold on for the ride.

Please do let me know what you think and drop me a line: altonya@lovealtonya.com

Blessings,
Al
www.lovealtonya.com

The Layers Series continues next with the full length release:
"Layers of the Past"

An AlTonya Exclusive

Made in the USA
Lexington, KY
30 December 2010